Guilty

Other books by the author

plays
Playmurder
The Dressing Gown

play anthologies
Painted, Tainted, Sainted
This Unknown Flesh

plays in anthologies
Lola Starr Builds Her Dream Home
Capote at Yaddo

poetry in anthologies
Eight Technologies of Otherness
Carnival: A Scream in High Park Reader
Plush
The Last Word
*Desire, High Heels and Red Wine: a collection by four gay
and lesbian writers*
Queeries: an anthology of gay male prose

Guilty

Sky Gilbert

a misFit
b o o k

INSOMNIAC PRESS

Edited by Michael Holmes/a misFit book
Copy edited by Lloyd Davis & Liz Thorpe
Designed by Mike O'Connor

Canadian Cataloguing in Publication Data

Gilbert, Sky, 1952-
        Guilty

ISBN 1-895837-29-4

I. Title.

PS8563.I4743G84 1998   C813'.54   C98-930293-X
PR9199.3.G54G84 1998

The publisher gratefully acknowledges the support of the
Ontario Arts Council.

Printed and bound in Canada

Insomniac Press, 393 Shaw Street,
Toronto, Ontario, Canada, M6J 2X4
www.insomniacpress.com

For Richard and Lynn and Michael:
You made me do it.
And special thanks to Dr. Ann Madigan.

Confess! He had to confess every sin. How could he utter in words to the priest what he had done? Must, must. Or how could he explain without dying of shame? Or how could he have done such things without shame? A madman, a loathsome madman! Confess! O he would indeed to be free and sinless again!

— James Joyce, *A Portrait of the Artist as a Young Man*

It seems to me that I must have killed someone. I know that sounds pretentious. As if I'm trying to be dangerous or something. But I really don't think there's any point in trying to be dangerous. I don't even know if I am, technically speaking, dangerous. It's just that everything seems to be pointing to the undeniable fact that I have, at some point in my life, killed someone.

Do you know how it is when dreams turn real? I mean, when you dream something over and over again, and you wake up in the middle of the night, thinking, "Is this a dream?" And other times, you're in the dream and you're thinking, "Hey this is only a dream, no need to get upset!" But, until you wake up at least, it's not a dream at all, it's reality. And then you start having those days when you wake up, and it doesn't seem like a dream — it seems like it really happened. And then the reality of what was once a dream begins to invade your life. And what started out as a dream is now something that really happened.

Or then again, maybe it had really happened, all along.

Of course it could all just be a nicotine fit.

I stopped smoking a week and a half ago and it just seems that my friends are all so evil about it. I mean, people I know who gave up smoking years ago started smoking the *moment* I stopped. And then they smoke in front of me. A non-smoking ex-boyfriend (he broke up with me years ago *because* I smoked) just lit up in front of me last night! "Oh, sorry!" he said, as I started to clean up the kitchen like crazy, just for something to do. And then there are those people who look at you and smile and say, "It'll be like this for another three years." Three years of anxiety attacks and depression and furious activity? Oh sure, that should be okay. I can handle that.

So it could just be the fact that I need a cigarette and I'm never ever going to have one again. That *could* have contributed to this feeling. Besides, all the evidence points to it.

I just don't want you to think that I'm starting this whole thing out in this way to be sort of like Camus, or something. You know, "My father died today, or was it yesterday?" I mean, I'm not alienated; I'm not a *symbol* of alienation. And this is not a novel, anyway. It's a pamphlet. It's an exploration of my guilt.

I think it's important to tell you about Cassidy.

He's certainly related in some way to this whole "Am I a murderer?" thing. Now, I'm not sure if I murdered Cassidy or not. I sure haven't seen him around for a while. Which is unusual, for me, as you'll see. (Although there *is* something very murderable about

Cassidy. That is, Cassidy is certainly a ripe candidate for murder. But the jury is still out on whether or not I murdered him — I doubt it. But...)

I certainly hurt him, I guess. If he was capable of being hurt. Which I think he was, underneath all that — whatever.

I met Cassidy at the baths. Which is really absolutely the right place to meet someone like him. He was a little bit chubby, in the nicest way. Blond, boyish. Very much my type. He had sort of a sulky look about him, and a plump, tan-lined, fuckable ass (I never fucked it). He was probably in his late twenties; a fading hustlerboy. Very Andrew Cunanan.

In fact once he told me that he hustled now and then. It was a *major* confession. I had to kiss him and stroke him and make it better afterwards. It was a very big deal for him to tell me that he fucked for money. For me it was just erotic, imagining him sucking dick, taking it up the ass like the little blond sexpig he was. Yeah, very erotic. Anyway, I found his big confession sort of touching because he didn't think I'd love him any more if I knew he was a hooker, when all it actually did was give me a hard-on. I mean, I've always had a thing for hookers anyway — they bring out the worst in me. (And the best.) I love them all because basically, let's face it, if you're a hooker, you're a sexual person. Now by that I don't mean that you *choose* to be a sexual person. Not necessarily. No, not that. You just are, one way or the other. Sex is a big part of your life. And sex was a very big part of Cassidy's life. In fact sometimes I don't know why I'm not a hooker, I sure love sex enough.

Anyway, Cassidy was this cute little cuddly guilty hooker boy and we used to fuck at the baths. Or more precisely, suck. Wow could that boy suck. Shit. I mean there are people who are just born to suck cock. Their mouths are just made that way. And Cassidy was like that. Quite the little cocksucker he was. Only truly happy when he had it in there, like a baby bottle or a soother. I remember his big eyes looking up at me, his big blue eyes, very daddyboy.

You know, it was all very incestuous.

By incestuous I mean it was basically clear, when we were having sex, that I was molesting him. That's what Cassidy wanted, to be molested. What do I mean by that? Well you see, Cassidy actually *had* been molested as a child. He made that very clear. He told me early on. Said that some schoolteacher had raped him and he was still very hurt by it. Not only hurt, but angry. And he vowed that he was going to get the guy; take him to court. And he did. After I stopped dating him I saw an article in the Focus section of the paper and sure enough Cassidy had succeeded in taking this guy to court and winning. I think he got him fired or something. I don't think he actually got any money. Cassidy never, ever, had any money.

So molestation figured largely in Cassidy's life and I have to say it's sort of what attracted me to him. I mean, when we were having sex he'd look up at me with his big baby-blue eyes, my dick just about to go into his mouth, and he'd say, "You won't hurt me, will you? Promise me you won't hurt me?" That's what he'd say. Now for me, this was sort of a challenge. I know it sounds strange, but I don't think I'm alone in this.

I remember living next door to this girl, she was sort of retarded or mentally fucked up in some way, and she used to stare at me all the time on my balcony. One day I got locked out of my apartment and our balconies were sort of adjoining, and I asked if I could go through her apartment and she said, "Okay, but you won't rape me, will you?" And it just occurred to me that *that* was a pretty provocative thing to say. I mean, it never would have occurred to me to rape her. First of all she wasn't that cute (sorry, but it's true), and second, *I'm gay* for fucksake, I can't think of anything less appealing than raping a woman.

But it struck me that if she had said that to some straight asshole, I mean, some violent straight fuck trying to prove his masculinity (the way those straight guys always are), then he might have just gone and raped her, no matter what she looked like. I'm not saying that she deserved to be raped. But I am saying that she was asking for it, literally. Which seems to me a pretty dangerous thing.

Now the thing with Cassidy is, whenever he said, "You won't hurt me, will you?" and looked at me like that, something deep down inside of me told me that he wanted me to hurt him. How do I know? Well, first of all, you just had to hear him say it and look at his eyes.

Then there were other clues.

Like the fact that he was always a bit bruised. One way or the other. He always had a bit of a cut somewhere on his eye or a bit of black and blue on his neck, which I just thought meant he was into rough sex. And he definitely was. But the other clue was that he was always telling me about the way ex-boyfriends beat him up. Yeah, he always talked about that. And it was with fear and trepidation and everything, but after he had told me over and over about how this ex-boyfriend had just started punching him one day outside Starbucks, and like he must have told me this story ten times, well, it just seemed to me that Cassidy was just trying to get me to hit him or something. So one day I asked him. I said, "Cassidy…" (I think I was sitting on him in bed at the time, with my dick in his face), "Cassidy, you don't want me to beat you up, do you? Because listen, I'm not going to beat you up, whatever you say. I'm never going to beat you up. I'm not that kind of guy."

At least I didn't think I was that kind of guy.

But two things. I did hit Cassidy. I mean, just a little bit, just in bed, for fun. But I did hit him. I'm not saying that I, you know, knocked him out, nothing like that. But, I'd sit on him and slap him around. Gently. Come to think of it, some of those bruises — I guess I *could* have caused them. I say *could* because it's unlikely. Unless he was very easily bruised. Because I never hit him hard, I just did it for fun. As a sort of sexual game, because I knew he liked it. Mind you, when I was hitting him, he was saying, "No, no, don't hit me!" But in a playful sort of way, you know what I mean?

And the other thing is, after I'd known Cassidy for a while I began to realize why people might really want to hit him. Hard. Why people might just want to take a good whack at him. Because he was nuts. Totally looney. A kind of walking, talking Jerry Springer episode. I mean, there was so much stupid shit going on his life. Full of melodrama. And he was a bit of a stalker. Loved to phone you and phone you until you wanted to bash his head in. That's why I never took him to my place. I didn't want him to know where I lived.

All this is leading up to the fact that, well, Cassidy was beaten up. Almost killed really, and they never caught the guy.

So anyway. As for the melodrama, it's hard to explain, but every time I'd meet Cassidy for a drink or whatever there'd be some sort of crisis. Some sort of problem in his life that sounded like it was right off TV. Like he'd say, "My sister's boyfriend's a coke addict and he just attacked my mother so I have to go stay with her." Or he'd say, "My ex-boyfriend just got out of prison and he keeps trying to get into my apartment so I have to get the locks changed." Or, "I only have one kidney and I have to get the other one taken out and then I'm going to Key West to recuperate. This should all happen next week." He was full of weird stuff like that and I think most of it was untrue. At least, in some respect (though there was some truth in it, too). I mean, he never went to Key West; not when I knew him. But it always seemed there was some major *thing* going on, real or imagined, and after a while, it didn't make much difference — it was all just trouble. I mean, once I was lying in his bed after he sucked me off and the intercom buzzed. He answered it and so I said, "Who's that?" And he said, "Oh that's my sister's cokehead ex-con husband and he's coming up to talk to me." So of course I asked, "About what?" And Cassidy said he "wasn't sure." And I said, "I'm sure as hell not staying in this fucking bed." I mean, it seemed to me a sure bet that his fucked up brother-in-law was not going to be a big fan of homosexuals in general. Because even though I'm a very big guy I'm also a fucking coward. So I bounded out of bed and got dressed. Cassidy actually went down to the door and met this psycho while I sat in the lobby in a pair of shorts and watched the whole thing. And sure enough Cassidy was talking to some guy in a muscle car. But it could have been his own drug dealer, for Christsakes: it could have been anybody.

This is an example of the kind of shit that happened to Cassidy all the time.

Once I actually said, "Cassidy, couldn't we just have a date? A date just like normal people?" And he goes, "What do you mean?" And so I say, "You know, a date where we go see a movie or to a club and then have a soda or something. No ex-cons and no kidney failure and no mothers dying of heart attacks. Just a date." I think he was offended. Or he didn't really know what I was talking about.

So anyway, the time I should really get to, the time that is relevant to all this stuff, is the time when Cassidy was seriously beaten up and I was implicated. For quite awhile. Seriously implicated.

Because I was with him at the time.

Not exactly at *the* time. Not at the time he was attacked. But the night *of* it. Let's put it this way, I definitely was not responsible for the way he was allegedly beaten up.

See, it went like this.

Cassidy and I were having a date. Everything was pretty normal, as I remember. He was trying to tell me about his latest melodrama and I think that was the night when I was sort of yelling at him, saying couldn't we just have a routine date. And he goes, "Well, these things are happening to me, I'm sorry." So I said, "Don't be sorry that there's shit in your life, but tonight can't we just look at the trees or something?" Anyway, we ended up outside this theatre. In fact it was a theatre I was going to be performing in (so I had keys). That's me: actor, performer, drag queen, gay activist. In fact I'm kinda famous. In my own eensie stupid gay snipey little faggot community, I'm famous. Though I don't know why they call it a goddamn community, since it's so evil and fucked — but that's another story. You'll have to wait.

So this theatre was where I was soon to be starring

and I was going to be a big shit and hopefully get rave reviews for my marvellous performance as a "fop." (It was a Restoration Comedy: I always get the gay parts — they call them fops, or the madman, or the friend, or the "witty man about town" — but they're all just fag parts. It's hard to explain if you're not gay. If you look at old movies and stuff, you can tell the gay parts, even if the characters are not effeminate. It's always the character outside the action, a little wacky, usually someone's friend, who comments on the action. Someone who doesn't have a love life *in the play*, because their love life would be too disgusting for the patrons. Sometimes, in old French plays, this character used to work out the whole plot in his head and explain it to the audience. They called him the "*Raisonneur*." And you'll see that, even to this day, even when they make a gay movie, the *really* gay characters still have minor roles in terms of the main action. I mean, when I get asked to be in a gay film or play, for instance, I still get the same part. The leading characters are gay, but they're very straight-acting and they're always played by nice straight actorboys who never touch their assholes and work out at the gym and have perfect hair. These guys, of course, are full of goodwill about being in a gay play or movie. And they go on TV and talk about how difficult it is to "stretch" themselves for the role. The raging faggots — like me — get to play, you'll never guess, raging faggots! Let me tell you, even in this day of gay plays and movies, the real faggot characters still live upstairs and pop down in their undies for witty effeminate conversation and plot disentanglement. I'm not knocking it. I get paid a lot for being wise and effeminate and a little bit nuts. Oh yeah, and dying. I'm usually dying in these movies. But I keep a brave face.

And I trade brilliant quips with my nurse about Judy Garland and stuff. Don't get me started here or I'll drive you nuts.) Now, the crew was still working, and the set was still under construction, and I thought: "Wow, that would be a great place to take Cassidy and fuck his mouth."

I should explain that I have a bit of a thing about construction sites. Anywhere there's pieces of wood lying around and they're building something big. I always have, ever since I was a kid. No, I don't think it's the construction workers. It's the sites themselves. They make me hard. I think it comes from an early sexual experience. When I was a kid I used to know this other kid, Robert Steck (great name, eh?), and his father was a builder of some kind. And once I went to visit Robert in this unfinished house and Robert suggested we run around the unfinished house with our little white asses showing and our little pricks dangling between our legs. Which we did. It was ever so fucking exciting. And afterwards, like a *dick*, I told my mother about it and said, "Mom, do you think I should have done that?" (Because I was such a goddamn guilty kid— still am.) And my mother said: *Don't you ever ever do anything like that again in your life do you hear me? Do you hear your mother?* So like naturally, because my mother made it something evil, punishable by death practically, it's something which gives me an enormous hard-on even to this day. Just *thinking* about unfinished buildings makes me hard.

So considering my erotic background, it seemed like just the thing to do with Cassidy: take him into the basement of the theatre, under this new contraption they were building, and shove my dick in his mouth. He was all funny about it: "I don't know if I wanna, I don't know if we should." But we did. There were some people there, when we came in, but they were just leaving, finishing working on the set for the play. I said "Hi" to them and everything, which made me very horny (it was all so sneaky, what we were doing!). And then we waited for them to leave, which they did almost immediately, thank God. I told them we had to pick up a script or something. And then I took Cassidy downstairs underneath the stage, which was so goddamn sexy, whipped out my dick, and, *fuck*. My dick never seemed so big, and he never seemed to be quite so desperate about begging for it. He was trying to talk to me with his mouth full. Which is like one of the sexiest things in the world. I wouldn't let him. I probably slapped him a couple of times and then I came all over his face.

He was very grateful.

Then he walked me home. And he really, like *really*, wanted to come home with me and stay the night, but I said no. Like I said, I thought Cassidy was a stalker and I wasn't about to let him know my apartment number yet. So I said good-bye to him, it must have been about 10 p.m., and he was going to walk home to his apartment which was a coupla blocks away.

Anyway, I go to bed and start thinking, "What a nice little sex scene, but shit, I've got to stop seeing Cassidy." I mean, you can't date a guy you're afraid to bring up to your apartment. It's not right.

Then I turned off the phone so my drunk sleep would be peaceful and I slept like a baby all night. Next morning I wake up and check my messages. And there are like one hundred messages on my phone. All from Cassidy. First one: "Jack, answer the phone, please answer the phone. Some guy just beat me up. He tried to kill me! Jack where are you?" And then: "Jack answer the phone please answer the phone I'm bleeding!" Stuff like that and then, finally, "Jack, I just went to the hospital because I was attacked. The police are here and I just wanted to warn you that they'll probably be calling you. Bye."

The police will probably be calling you. Bye. The police will probably be calling you. The police will probably be...

I can't tell you how that freaked me out. I mean, for a guy like me, a guy who's always been, well, guilty (I know I'm guilty, you'll see how guilty I am later), to have the police question me and to have to wait for the damn thing to happen — fuck, it was hell. So I called Cassidy immediately and asked him what happened.

And this was his story:

He said that he had gone directly home after I fucked his face and that he was so drunk he forgot to lock his door. Now this is the first part of the story which is, like, totally unbelievable, because Cassidy had, like, ten ex-boyfriends who wanted to rip his face apart. And because his sister's psycho boyfriend was a cokehead ex-con, he had at least five different kinds of locks on his door. I'm not kidding. His silly apartment was like a maximum-security prison. So it seemed very unlikely to me that Cassidy would forget to lock five locks. I mean, we're not talking a little slip-the-little-thing-into-the-whatchamacallit. We're talking *five* locks. So, first unbelievable thing, he forgot to lock his door. Then he collapses drunk on his bed and while he's drunk asleep some guy opens the door of his apartment, ties him up, rapes him, then strangles him and leaves him for dead.

Okay, I don't know. For me this story had a lot of stuff in it that was hard to swallow. First — what I said before — about not the locking the door. Then, the fact that Cassidy was so drunk that some guy could tie him up. Of course, maybe this was a big guy. (But Cassidy likes big guys, he likes big guys tying him up; I mean, *we* never did that, but we *could* have.) And then Cassidy gets raped, which I'm sure is possible, though this is going to sound horrible, especially if you transpose the genders here. But I mean, Cassidy was a little slut. Hey, I'm sure he'd been fucked before. I mean people paid him for it. He wanted me to fuck him even though he kept saying, "Don't fuck me, please don't fuck me." All I'm saying is, for a guy like that, what's the use of struggling and getting all bloody and everything? Why not just let yourself get fucked? I mean, if you're going to let some trick fuck you, why cause yourself trouble if this guy just doesn't happen to be paying?

I know that's probably not fair. I guess whether you're a hooker or not you don't want somebody's dick up your asshole if you don't want it there.

Anyway. Cassidy was raped. And then the guy strangled him so hard that he was left for dead. Except, the next day when I saw him he just had the usual coupla bruises. I mean, he didn't look bad at all. Maybe a little more bruised up. But *left for dead*? Seems to me, if you were left for dead, you should be in the hospital for a week.

But no, not my bouncy little masochist pal.

So, whether I believed his story or not, I was going to be questioned by the police. And I didn't know what I was going to be questioned about. I assumed I was a suspect. I mean, I had been with Cassidy that night, and I had stuck my dick in his mouth. Why couldn't it have been me who beat him up? They probably thought it *was* me.

So I was kind of in a state. Here I was, ready to open as a big star in this play, making my thousandth debut as a witty fop, and at the same time, some little hooker was having me questioned about his left-for-dead strangulation. It made me nervous.

I lost a lot of sleep about those cops. It scared the shit out of me. What the fuck was I supposed to tell them? Should I tell them Cassidy had sucked me off that night but that I didn't go home with him because I was afraid he was a stalker? I don't know, it seemed to me that there was stuff about our relationship (which by now I was referring to as a coupla dates, because that's what it was really, a coupla dates) that straight people, especially cops, would not understand.

So anyway, the fateful day came, and I'm at work (it was two days before opening night and we were rehearsing with the very contraption just inches above where Cassidy and I had done the dirty), and the police are there. And this is the thing. This is the killer. It's not a couple of big burly cop guys. No, it's a coupla women. *Women.*

Now I've got nothing against women, but this was too weird. I mean, with big cute fat-assed brutal dumb straight cops — you know, the usual kind that read the *Sun* and kick the dog — my guard is up because I, well, I just figure that guys like that are the enemy, you know. Especially when they're wearing a uniform. So if I'm dealing with a cop who is a straight guy, no problem. I'm all closed up. He's not getting in.

But a woman cop? That's completely different. I mean, my mother was a woman. I told all my secrets to my mother. I told her horrible stuff no one has ever heard. And she forgave me for it. So you bring a mother-type character (I mean, I don't see women as sexual so I tend to see them sometimes as mother types, which I know is fucked, but what can I say?) and a guy like me is going to confess. Confess everything.

Confess things he didn't even fucking do, for Christsakes.

So they meet me in the green room (the place where you wait and get nervous before the show — appropriate, eh?). Did you see *Fargo*? Well that's the idea, they totally reminded me of Frances McDormand. Both of them. I mean they weren't in uniform. Just wearing nice little skirts and loose tops. Nothing sleazy or anything. Very businesslike. Not attractive but not ugly. Just completely innocent-looking. The type who could make you confess to the fucking TWA disaster or the Atlanta Olympic bombing.

So we go into the green room and all the time I'm quaking in my boots, literally. And there are all the posters for all these arty plays all over the walls — what do they think of that? They probably feel totally out of place but they aren't showing it; no, not showing it at all. So they just sit there and talk to me. Smiling a lot, cracking jokes, being chummy. *Respecting* me. (I was a big actor and, as I said, I had been active in the gay community.) It was fucking chilling. I think you get my drift. It would have been so much easier if they were threatening. But no.

So they ask me about Cassidy and the night we spent together and I told them I brought him to the empty theatre and that we necked (*necked!*), because I just couldn't imagine them understanding what really happened. And they just smiled and nodded and took notes. They could have been fucking meter maids.

Then they asked me about Cassidy, and I could see that I probably wasn't really under suspicion. At least I think they wanted me to believe I wasn't under suspicion. It was Cassidy they were suspicious of, like he had beaten himself up or something. They were like, "Would you consider Cassidy, well, someone who liked to party?" Someone who liked to *party*? "Fuck, I don't know how to tell you ladies, but this guy was a screaming, on-his-back, legs-wiggling-in-the-air, 24-hour hooker masochist sexpig." Only I couldn't say that. I didn't feel it would be fair to Cassidy. Besides, straight people — male or female — just have different attitudes about sex. I mean, to straight people — hooker/women and sexpig/faggots are just like another race. Straight people treat them the way they would probably treat pond scum. You have to be very careful around straight people in power. You can't be really sexual with them unless you want to drive them crazy (which sometimes I like to do) because they just get so hysterical. So the important thing with these two sweet coppers was to just say I "necked" with Cassidy, like he was my sweet little boyfriend or something. They could understand that. Fuck, they'd probably just imagine the rest. Straight people, that's one thing about them, they have very good imaginations. (I think it's because a lot of them don't fuck that much. But all this stuff about straight people is hearsay because I'm not one myself. They *claim* not to fuck much... which would mean they use their imaginations a lot. Sorry if it sounds like I'm treating straight people like they're another race, with a separate culture and everything. But to be perfectly honest, to me, they are. I used to have this great dyke friend — Lou — who told me that she always just expected the whole world to be gay, and believed it, unless proven wrong. An optimist. All I know is, straight people are like aliens. They have different mating habits, customs, and everything. Actually sometimes I think they have some of the same sexual habits we do, it's just that they lie more about it. Straight women, for instance. Most of them are just so terrified of being called whores they just keep their mouths shut, even when their legs are wide open.)

So I told them that Cassidy liked to party — "Moderately." Which was so fucking nice of me (such a big lie). But then all I needed was for Cassidy to come back to me saying that the cops had said that I said that he beat *himself* up when he was drunk. I mean, if anyone was capable of strangling themselves almost to death it was Cassidy. But at this point I didn't want the cops *or* Cassidy mad at me. I had this fantasy actually that this entire thing was just a plot Cassidy had dreamed up to make me pay attention to him. I know it sounds crazy. But this whole thing was insane anyway. Of course, the weirdest thing was, after the police visited me for the first time, I began to feel that maybe I *did* beat up Cassidy.

Call me fucked, but that's always been one of my problems. Hey, if there's a crime around, I probably committed it. Somebody did something bad? Hey, I'm guilty. You know, like when the teacher always used to say, "No one is leaving this classroom until someone admits to shitting in the pool!" or whatever other goddamn thing happened? Well, I'd be the guy that would raise his hand and say, "Yeah it's me, I did the dirty. That's my juicy log down there disintegrating in the chlorine." And then they'd go in there, right, with forensic DNA testing and stuff, and test the turd, and it wouldn't be my turd at all, and everybody would look at me like why is he so crazy, trying to claim some human waste that wasn't his own? But that's me. Something bad happened? I probably did it.

So this is just to explain, because, you know, I definitely did not strangle Cassidy. I want to make that clear. But for some reason I began to feel like I did. And then we get to the whole Christian thing.

Which I think is very important. I mean, I used to be a Christian. I was almost a fucking minister and...

Well, maybe I should tell you this story.

When I went for my catechism, you had to take these classes with the minister (we were Anglican). And there I was talking to him and I just felt I had to ask, "What about this virgin birth shit? I mean I want to believe in it, but it just seems so unlikely, you know?" And the minister agreed with me. He was a nice guy, but he had his limits. He gave me some half-assed explanation about the virgin birth that didn't explain anything to a horny thirteen-year-old, and then he said: "Have you ever thought of becoming a minister?" And I said, "Why?" And he said, "Well, you're the only one who is taking this process seriously. You're the only one who asks me any questions." Which is pretty sad, when you think about it. I mean, the only guy he could think of as a likely candidate for the clergy was an atheist and a future homosexual and God knows what else.

So I always remember the time when this priest asked me if I wanted to be a minister and think that, well, I come from a pretty religious background. And one of the things I remember being taught in church was that if you thought a thing it was as bad as doing it. In other words, thinking an evil thought was as bad as doing an evil deed. Now if we apply this whole theory to me and Cassidy, then things get pretty dense.

I mean, okay, I didn't fuck and strangle Cassidy. But I fucked his face and I slapped him around. And Cassidy was such a little fuckhead I often did want to strangle him. I could sympathize with the guy who beat him up outside Starbucks. And if I had kept seeing Cassidy I bet I *would* have ended up raping him.

He was sure pushing me, always telling me not to and then waving his little ass in my face.

So what I'm saying is that, according to Christ (and he's the big cheese, right?), you're always guilty. Just thinking about something makes you guilty. So according to this definition I raped and strangled Cassidy and left him for dead. If you believe what the Son of God says, I'm guilty.

I know I'm hard on myself sometimes. But the thing is, you've got to be. Maybe it's my religious upbringing, I don't know. But I think we're all guilty in some way. And if we say we're not, then we're hiding something. Something very bad that just leads to worse stuff. Sometimes I get pretty overwhelmed by how bad I am. And it isn't just Christianity or my upbringing; it's everything everywhere that says so.

Like Hollywood. I was brought up on years of Hollywood movies that say exactly the same thing. My favourite movie, for instance (but it's also the one I hate the most — I hate it so much I can't watch it; even though I do watch it, over and over again) is *A Place in the Sun,* with Montgomery Clift and Elizabeth Taylor and Shelley Winters. I'm sure you've seen the movie — yeah, it's one of the big ones.

The story goes like this. Montgomery Clift is caught between two classes of people; he's the son of this poor religious woman from Missouri, but he comes from rich Eastman stock. And these Eastmans have scored a lot of money making bathing suits. That's the one comical thing about the movie, actually. I mean, the first thing he sees when he comes to the big city is a big poster of this beautiful woman wearing a bathing suit. And Elizabeth Taylor, his one true love, is always wearing bathing suits, and the one thing in his life he always wants is (a place in the sun) to sit around in a bathing suit with Elizabeth Taylor drinking martinis, and that's what gets him into so much trouble. It's like, in this movie, bathing suits are the root of all evil. Which I can see is sort of true, if you think of the world in a certain way.

Anyway, he comes to the big city and gets a job in the bathing suit factory and meets this sort of homely girl (played by Shelley Winters) and he just sort of wants to get his rocks off with her and he does and she gets pregnant. At the same time he starts this affair with Elizabeth Taylor, who is completely rich and beautiful and perfect. She's the one he's really in love with, of course. But the dumb ugly girl Shelley is pregnant and this is driving him crazy because he doesn't want to marry her. So one day he takes her out to a lake in a boat and, this is the key, he doesn't actually murder her, but he murders her in his mind. That is, he wants to hit her with a paddle (and who wouldn't, I mean Shelley Winters is a lot like Cassidy — very whiny and pitiful and always going on about her miserable life — I mean, fuckable on one level but ultimately sort of glum). It's the classic thing: there are people you fuck in the dark when you are horny, and there are people who you want everyone to *know* you're screwing because they are so beautiful and glamorous. Which is sort of fucked but that's the way it is sometimes. So anyway, Montgomery is out with Shelley in this rowboat and he wants to murder her but he doesn't exactly, he just doesn't save her when she falls out. And of course after that he does everything wrong. Instead of running back to the police and saying, "Oh shit. My pregnant girlfriend just fell out of the boat! Do something!" — instead of that, he runs back to Elizabeth Taylor and goes for a ride with her in her swell car. Then he goes on trial for murder and Raymond Burr is the prosecuting attorney. And because Raymond Burr played Perry Mason on TV you know for sure Montgomery's goose is cooked. Montgomery gets convicted and he goes to the electric chair and at the end the priest convinces him that, even though he didn't actually hit her with a paddle, he wanted to, and that's the same thing.

And the priest is right, I think. Certainly that's what the movie thinks. I mean, even though *A Place in the Sun* was originally called *An American Tragedy* and adapted from this huge boring novel by Theodore Dreiser (I never bothered to read it, but I'm sure it's very boring), and even though I'm sure it's supposed to be about social injustice and how poor Montgomery Clift was caught between two social classes and that the shame of pregnancy and sex among the lower classes is a problem, I still think the movie is just about how we're all just guilty because we all have horrible thoughts. Which makes it a very difficult movie to watch. I mean, I totally identify with Montgomery Clift. And he is such a fucking good actor. Everybody is good. Shelley Winters is so cloying. (Did you ever see the parody that Carol Burnett did of the big scene? Oh, she was great. Sitting at the end of the rowboat whining and being such an ugly case that Harvey Korman just *had* to hit her with a paddle.) And Elizabeth Taylor is so beautiful she almost makes me want to stop being a homosexual. No, let's put it this way: she *is* a beautiful boy, that's how gorgeous she is in that movie. (You know, before her tits just got out of hand she was so gorgeous.) But Monty Clift just outdoes them all: he is *so* guilty. And the best scenes are after he's killed whiny Shelley and he's hugging Elizabeth Taylor and he knows he's leading a double life (he's really a killer).

And she's going: "What's wrong, what's wrong?" And he can't tell her but he knows that all this happiness is just going to go away because he's guilty.

I guess one of the reasons the movie affects me so much is because I used to be straight. It's such a long story. Until I was twenty-eight years old I was completely heterosexual. If you can believe it. I mean, I had fantasies and everything, but basically I was practically living with my girlfriend. And my girlfriend was very much like Shelley Winters. Let me explain. She was really nice and everything, and even pretty. But she was also very depressed and fucked up and whiny. (Maybe she was just whiny with me because I didn't fuck her enough. I remember at the time, the big issue with me was, how many times is enough? Was once a week enough? Now I know that as soon as you have to worry if you're fucking somebody enough, you'd better stop fucking them.) And I wasn't in love with her. All the while I was dating her I knew inside myself that I was gay and I used to hoard all these dirty sex magazines like *Blueboy* and stuff and jerk off, and she found them once. It was very melodramatic, and she was upset at first but then I said, "I think I'm bisexual." And she said, "That's okay, we can work it out, we can fantasize together." And of course the last thing I wanted to do was fantasize about men with *her*. But I felt so sorry for her. I mean, I think she was in love with me and she tried so hard to understand. I think it's because she had a gay brother and she was kind of in love with him. Anyway, the whole thing went on and on and it probably would have gone on forever until I noticed my violent tendencies. You see, I threw a fork at her.

It was really very innocent. We were having an argument in my basement apartment, which adjoined hers, and it was all very claustrophobic and I got mad and threw a fork at her. It missed her, thank God, but it made me think, "Fuck, I threw a fork at my girlfriend." And I was throwing fits at these women at the McDonald's (where I worked part-time) and my friend Barb, she read my chart, and it said that she saw me surrounded by, and very involved with, tons and tons of men. So the fork and the fits and the chart and everything seemed to point to the fact that I was simply gay. Not to mention the magazines at the bottom of my filing cabinet.

But during this whole time I felt just like Montgomery Clift. I even had a glamorous, intellectual girlfriend who was sort of my Elizabeth Taylor. That was Barb. And I would go see Barb, who was a writer, and I was a burgeoning (I almost wrote bludgeoning) actor, and Barb and I used to have vicious intellectual chats. She was very beautiful and arty and smart and the exact opposite of my girlfriend. She was a writer and dating this gay writer she didn't know was gay. I think Barb was in love with me; we'd sit and get drunk and trash my girlfriend. Barb would ask, "Why are you going out with her, you have nothing in common?" And it was only later that I realized that's what all homosexuals do. You can always tell a closeted gay man: he's dating a woman he has nothing in common with. Then of course, he *has* to be unhappy and choose men. It happened to me. And of course my real girlfriend at the time would have been good enough to make any normal dumb straight guy happy. She was pretty and she liked to fuck, and she was nice. But of course, she wasn't unbelievably genius-smart and wild and wacky and sexually screwy, which is what I admire in a woman. All homosexuals admire brilliant wacky women who have trouble with men.

So I really admire Barb. But I had this really demented moment with her which really upset me once. Barb was also a visual artist (as well as being an actress and a writer — like a lot of my friends, she kind of did everything — it's the only way to stay alive these days, financially) and once I volunteered to pose nude for her. I will never forget this. I was and always have been shy about my body. Even though I am a total slut and I can go naked in any gay bar, I'm still very sensitive (call me a fucked-up fag), so it was a big deal for me to take my clothes off for Barb, but I thought I'd be liberated and try. So one day I went over to her place and stripped and lay down on the bed. And I did it a coupla times and everything was okay. But then one day I was lying on my stomach and Barb just stopped. Barb was Asian, though she was raised in Guyana and had this very prissy British way of talking. Very uptight (even though she wasn't; it was her brilliant trick). I'm sure that's why guys chased after her all the time. Straight guys *love* uptight girls (just to torture themselves or something). And by dating a gay man, Barb, who was really beautiful in an Asian way like Elizabeth Taylor, tortured them some more.

So beautiful Barb is drawing my ass as I'm lying on the bed and suddenly she stops and goes, "Sorry Jack, that's enough. Get dressed." And I said, "What? What's the matter?" And she goes: "Jack... really, I didn't want to see that, there's no need to do the spread shot for me, really." And honestly I was so embarrassed I didn't know what she was talking about, but she made me feel so dirty, dirtier than when I was naked with Robert Steck and my mother said, *Don't you ever ever do that again!* I mean, her revulsion was so intense I could almost taste it. I realized afterwards that I must have done some sort of spread beaver for her, you know, shown her the whole thing, all the way to China.

Now here we go again, it was such a Montgomery Clift moment. I don't remember if I really gave Barb the beaver shot when I was posing for her, but I can imagine that I would have *wanted* to, and that's the crux of it. I mean what gay man wouldn't? That's what it's all about, being gay. I mean you can try and dignify the whole thing and have gay political parties and churches and gay choirs and stuff like that, but what it's really all about is a man being really proud of his asshole. I mean like *really* proud. Loving it and spreading it and eating it and showing it to other people. Other gay men. Being asshole proud. That's the truth about being gay and don't let anyone tell you otherwise.

So probably in a subconscious way I was just into showing Barb the beaver. Even if I didn't mean to, or didn't actually do it, I knew inside I wanted to and it made me so ashamed. But Barb's reaction? Give me a break. I mean, she was not at all uptight about sex. She always told me about the men she fucked and how it went. So this was very strange and demented and upsetting. Anyway, I think this incident may have had something to do with me coming out — I mean, the fork and my horoscope and my fits and then showing the whole story — all the whole dirty story — to Barb.

During this period I was very guilty. I was kissing my girlfriend and even managing to fuck her (just like Montgomery Clift), but I was jerking off at night with my little *Blueboy* magazines and giving Barb the beaver shot. And it made me really guilty when people later said that my girlfriend went a little nuts for a while. I mean after we broke up. People said that she sort of became weird and got obsessed with gay men. And then she went litigation-crazy, suing people and stuff. And she got rich. Apparently she's okay now (thank God). Of course I felt this was all my fault because I had been her big boyfriend and I was like the biggest fag in town — and a bit famous too.

So that's a lot of guilt. But my obsession with *A Place In The Sun* is more than just about my ex-girl-friend. I think it's a bit about Cassidy. I think it's about the fact that I am guilty of something very big. Of killing someone maybe. I dunno.

(Oh yeah, one more movie that I can barely watch — but I always do — is *The Velvet Touch*. You just have to see it. With Rosalind Russell, a classic. It's this theatre movie, and being an actor myself I get so into it. She kills her producer because he's forcing her to be in frothy comedies when she wants to play Hedda Gabler. What motivation, eh? And she, like, hits him over the head with a Tony. Well it's not exactly a Tony, but some big theatre award statue, and she clobbers him with it. Then she spends the whole movie being guilty. Sydney Greenstreet is the cop. Oh it's wonderful. And he's really nice to her, just the way the cops were nice to me about Cassidy. But all the while she's his suspect. And the great thing is that she gets away with it. And then this really nice actress, who was actually in love with the producer Rosalind killed, gets blamed for it and dies because she feels so bad, and on her death bed she has a great scene where she says to Rosalind, something like, "How can you live with yourself?" And how can she? You don't know how Rosalind can live with such guilt, you just don't. Finally, you realize Rosalind can't live with it because she gets the part, the Hedda Gabler part, and

Sydney Greenstreet is watching from the wings. He's a policeman but also one of her fans. As she performs it, and you think that she's just so guilty that when Hedda kills herself on stage Rosalind is going to *really* shoot herself with the gun. But she doesn't, she gives herself up to Sydney because she can't stand the guilt. But she did get to play Hedda Gabler before she went to jail.

What a movie.)

But what I have to finally get to here is the point of this whole thing. This whole exploration. Which is to figure out whether or not I killed someone. And that's a tough one. But like I said, all the evidence points to it.

But before I tell you about the whole killing thing I think we have to get into motive, and this involves stuff that I find very hard to talk about. But I'm going to have to tell you this. In fact, you're probably not going to like hearing it. If you're squeamish, I would say, well, maybe it's time to turn back. Time to stop reading this. It gets pretty, literally, filthy and dis-gusting from now on. So look, I don't want any prudes going, "Oh this book is so filthy it should be banned." You know why? Because I warned you. I completely warned you (I'm doing it now), and if you don't want to read any more then just don't because I guarantee you're going to be grossed out. This is kind of, you know, the gates of hell, the crossing of the river Styx, or whatever it's called. So just imagine some kindly old white-haired guy like the angel in *It's A Wonderful Life* saying, "Now Laddie. Or Girlie. Now's the time to turn back. You still have time." And you can turn back. And if you're the type of person who just skipped the whole beginning of this thing to get to the so-called "good part," then you deserve everything you get. If I'm going to tell you why I think I'm guilty, then I have to tell you all of the bad things I did. Even the very worst.

The dangerous part, of course, is that some of you must have thought of doing these horrible things yourself. But most of you haven't. Most of you will just read this next part and say to yourself, "He's so horrible. I'm glad I'm not like that." Which is fine. I mean, that's what makes the whole world go round, right? Because it's very important for people to have people to hate, so they can feel better than them. Usually it's people from other countries or people of different colours (or just women in general), but a lot of times it's homosexuals or just sexual people. I know you might think I'm just being sarcastic, but I'm not. I really think that it is completely a trait of human nature to hate people that you think are smelly or disgusting or lower than you are. So, you know, if people like me are, like, perfectly willing to take on the responsibility of being the lowest of the low, well, why not? I'll be so disgusting to you that you can go through the natural human thing of being more secure in yourself. I have yet to meet a person who was so secure in themselves that they were happy without having to compare themselves to someone else. I mean, even Mother Teresa probably thought, now and then, "I'm so glad I'm not selfish like that other nun over there." I mean, of course she would have to, unless she was perfect. And I don't believe anyone is.

So here I am, an emotional masochist offering myself as an example of the most disgusting thing on earth. So start feeling superior to me now. Start warming up.

The thing is, I basically have a sort of a sexual fetish which I haven't told you about. It's really disgusting. (Fuck, even just writing the word is weird.) Basically, it's *shit*. To some degree, I have to admit, I'm into shit.

I'm sure you'll have two questions in reaction to this. Your first one will be: What does this mean, exactly? And the second one, of course, is gonna be: Why are you telling me all this?

I'll answer your second question first because it's easier and quicker, even though it won't make much sense right now. I'm telling you because, ultimately, after you hear the *whole* story, then this confession of what I'm into will become very relevant. It all has to do with proving my guilt or innocence and it's very complicated. (I know that sounds condescending — bear with me — but I have to admit to the whole thing if there's any possibility of proving my inno-cence. I don't think it's really possible, but...)

So, to answer the first question. Well, it's the scat thing. (Before I tell you about scat I have to tell you one more thing which seems to indicate that I am permanently guilty. And this is true. When I was thirteen years old I was just wracked with guilt because I had this phrase repeating over and over in my head and I didn't know why. The phrase was: "I HATE GOD." Can you believe it? I was so upset. I told my mother and everything. I went to her and said, "Mom, what does this mean? I think I might hate God." And she said she didn't know what it meant. And, to tell you the truth, I didn't know what it meant either. I just knew that I was obsessed with the idea. What if I did hate God? What did that make me? Actually, I think this whole confession about scat might have something to do with hating God. Or maybe it's the opposite. Like, if you believe God includes all bodily functions and that nothing is disgusting, then loving God would mean loving your shit. I guess. But if you're like most people you think one of God's big things is to make sure you poop in the right place. So what I'm about to tell you puts me completely in the category of God haters.)

So scat. What is scat? For gay guys, it's not jazz singing, let me tell you. It's basically the love of poo and shit and turds and stuff. Now my love is not incredibly extreme and I have no idea where it started. And it has *nothing* to do with me being gay. My God, if you start on that I'll be very irritated. And I'm not contradicting myself. I know I said before that being gay was all about loving your asshole. Let me tell you it's a big step from loving your asshole to loving your shit. I mean the corollary (that's my best big word!) would be — if you love a woman's vagina then you should love to drink her piss. I know that *piss* does not come *out* of the vagina, I'm not that stupid, but it comes from the same area, and I'm just saying, that to claim all hets love girlpiss because they love vaginas is just the same as saying all fags love shit because they lick assholes. They don't. Let me tell you. There's not many of us. Sometimes I wish there were more.

So when did it all start? When did it...? Well, I'm sure it started with toilet training, but I'm not going to blame my goddamn mother. That's all everybody ever does. Blame their mother. Now maybe she was a bit severe with the porta-potty, but so what. Why shouldn't she be? Who wants some dirty kid shitting on the floor? It's embarrassing to have your kid make a mess, so I completely understand. But her strictness *may* have had something to do with it, Dr. Freud.

Or maybe not. The first time I noticed I was sort of into shit was when I read this great porn story in *Drummer*, which is this really neat gay leather magazine. I mean, sometimes it's great. Often it's just boring, but sometimes the stories are just the limit. I mean, one time I read this story about two guys who were having their balls tortured in a competition (they were tied up) and their balls were being slowly tacked onto a table (that's the skin, not the balls themselves or they'd die, stupid!). I found it enormously sexy. And the other story I found enormously sexy was the story of this boy who was forced to be a sexpig at this giant dinner. Oh my God, it was sexy.

So they tied up this boy's hands and feet and put him under the table at this dinner and he's supposed to suck off everybody at the table while they're eating. This, to me, is so sexy: the guys are just eating away and there's this kid under the table sucking them off and now and then they just go "Excuse me" or something, and they come or maybe one of them moans a bit while helping himself to a bit more potatoes. And I imagine all the guys around the table are big and hairy and probably a little bit smelly (but in a positive way).

So the guys are eating and the boy is sucking them off, getting a mouthful of cum each time. And pretty soon the guys are finished eating and now some of them feel like taking a shit. So what do you think happens? Sure, right. These guys just turn around (or more like, they've got holes in their chairs) and the boy just scurries under and they feel free to just drop a load in this boy's mouth.

Now I remember jerking off to this story a hundred

times and each time I came to the dropping the load in the boy's mouth part of the story I always used to come (but I will admit, sometimes I just couldn't read it).

Now let me make this clear. I have never eaten anybody's shit. And I don't think I ever want to. I can't imagine doing it. I don't even like the smell of shit very much. But there's something about taking a shit, or some boy taking a shit, that I find very sexy. Don't ask me why (and please, don't blame my mother).

So how has this fantasy manifested itself in my real life? Well... not much. Except that I did see this guy for a while who was really into shit, and he definitely wanted me to take a shit on him. I never did it though. I just couldn't. In fact, I knew *two* guys who wanted me to shit on them. At one time it seemed that's what everybody wanted from me on a date. And of course, I have definitely eaten some fine ass in my life, and now and then when you're eating ass, of course, you're going to run into a little bit of the stuff. And if I'm really hot for the kid (usually a really beautiful boy type) a little shit is not going to turn me off. Lots of these kids, their shit doesn't even stink. I'm talking about some fine eighteen-year-old. And that's what leads us to Cassidy. Cassidy's shit did not stink. Which was fucking amazing.

How did I know? Well, because I must have rimmed him a hundred times, and he must have sat on my face every night we were together. It was one of the things I really enjoyed. He loved it too. And even though he was very clean, now and then there'd be a little bit of you know what; and hey, I could handle it. I hardly even knew it was there.

But Cassidy and I also used to play some games that were a little more strange. For instance, Cassidy knew that I loved to blow him while I was sitting on the crapper. This is a favourite fantasy of mine. There I am, ass spread, with the wind from the plumbing blowing up my hole, and I'm blowing Cassidy. And usually, I'd also take a shit when I came (which was all very clean and everything, because I was, after all, on the crapper). This was one of the best things I did with Cassidy. And also, I used to sometimes make Cassidy take a shit while he was blowing me. This was a lot of fun. Because you know, Cassidy would whine and say, "No, please don't make me do that," and "I can't, I can't take a shit." And then I'd give him an enema and he'd look at me all wide-eyed and ask, "Do you really want me to do this? Does this really turn you on? Why does this turn you on?" Of course, these are unanswerable questions. But he did it. There was nothing like those little-boy eyes looking up at me as he took a shit. Made me come all over his face every time.

And once, I'll admit it, once I made Cassidy take a shit on the couch. That was... that was weird. You see, Cassidy had this white leather couch — probably not real leather, actually, and it was all in layers, like, if you want to know, it kind of looked like a pile of shit. Of white shit. And for some reason I really wanted Cassidy to take a shit on it. And one night he did for me. Imagine a nice firm brown turd just sitting there on his white couch. I also made him clean it up. I mean it was *his* shit.

(It's always reminded me of Fassbinder for some reason, the big filmmaker. I don't know if you've seen his films, but they are fabulous, even though the guy himself was so disgusting looking. I mean if anybody ever looked like he liked to eat shit it was Fassbinder. I know that sounds strange, but some people... you kind of know they're into shit. There's something about their smiles — you know, like the expression "shit-eating" grin — well, Fassbinder always looked to me like he had just chomped on some boy's load. And in this one interview with him, where he looks so old and smelly and greasy and disgusting, he's sitting on this gigantic couch which is all brown leather and looks like a pile of turds really, completely, and I bet if you asked Fassbinder he'd say, "Oh yeah, that's my turd couch. I like to watch the boys shit on it." I mean, the couch looks so much like a pile of shit. You just have to see this documentary to know what I mean.)

That's basically all I did with Cassidy in terms of shit. I know it might seem like a lot. But it was kind of the crux of this whole thing for me because, you see, Cassidy knew about that stuff. He knew what I was really into and what I liked to do. And for all his whining and moaning, he would do it. Everything I asked.

So that's when things started getting weird. Because the whole story of Cassidy isn't finished. When I said that the police came and questioned me about Cassidy's beating, well, they never found the guy who did it. And even though Cassidy and I never had sex again, that wasn't the end of our relationship. You can have a relationship with someone even if you never see them again. You can have a relationship with them if you just feel them around you or inside you and — I don't want to sound completely corny, — their energy, maybe, is still a part of you.

After the police questioned me about Cassidy getting strangled and almost killed, things got creepy. Life was a kind of limbo, in a Sydney Greenstreet sort of way. That is, I knew the police hadn't solved the whole thing because I didn't read about it in the papers. If they had solved it Cassidy very definitely would have been interviewed. He really liked publicity. They even posted a picture of the suspected rapist around the gay community. It didn't look like me, thank God. Can you believe it? I actually expected the guy to look like me. I thought, "That's the way they are going to get me to confess. They'll put up this picture of this guy that looks like me and I'll have to confess just to get them to take down the picture." Because as you might have guessed, I definitely have this thing about confessing. I'm not saying I go around confessing to things I didn't do. That's not my thing. I mean, I could be going on here about being guilty and then the whole thing might just be, "Oh yeah, surprise! I just like to confess and I'm confessing to something I didn't do." But it's not that simple. I'm pretty sure I know the difference between the truth and a lie. Most of the time.

But the thing is, I think the whole idea of confessing is like the major contribution of Catholicism to modern religion. I mean, if you're a Protestant, like I am, you're just guilty. Don't take my word for it. Just read up on some Protestant stuff. I remember when I was a kid I read this Lutheran book that was meant, believe it or not, for kids. This was at the house of a woman friend of my mother's. She was really pious and so were her kids — which made them very boring. But when I found this Lutheran book I couldn't fucking believe it. It said that everyone was born guilty — that's original sin — and that they would always be guilty for their whole life no matter what. Basically you had to die to stop being guilty. Which I don't get: I thought Jesus died for our sins. But not for Lutherans, no way, there's no getting out of it. I mean this whole book just said — *to kids* — you're bad. You'll always be bad so there's no way out. With this kind of reasoning, I figure, why not go out and rob a variety store, right, just for fun? Anyway, the book had a huge effect on me. My mother told me to ignore it, but that's like a judge saying: "Ignore the prosecution's remarks... strike them from the record." I mean big fucking deal, the jury's heard them already.

But what I think is great about the whole Catholic religious thing is that you can confess. I mean it's really wonderful. You can do all the dirty you want — jerk off, have incredible fantasies (even about shit and stuff) — and on Sunday you just go and confess and all is forgiven. And then you start over again. It's great actually: sin like mad so you can be really guilty and then really get forgiven. I know in my case, though, I have a primal religious guilt thing. I will just mention it now (not go into the whole thing), but basically I'm very sexually attracted to Jesus. I'm sorry, but it's true. Hey, I think a lot of people are, they just don't say so. I know this girl who did a whole play about it — I had a part in it, by the way (I played a priest, another gay role) — called *Screw Jesus!* It was all about how she was a young Catholic girl and she wanted to fuck Jesus. So I know I'm not alone in this. But with me there were basically two reasons for this Jesus attraction. First, I had a picture of him over my bed, and Christ, he was just so damned cute. You see this picture depicted Jesus as this really adorable white guy with blond streaks in his hair. I mean, he could have been Jewish, but it was highly unlikely. He was very non-Semitic and really, really pretty.

Actually, he looked a little like Cassidy. That is, if Cassidy had ever had a shred of self-respect or intelligence. And I've never really been attracted to Semitic or Italian types, just blonds. Even dyed blonds like Cassidy. They're the best kind actually. It's not a prejudice. I'm not saying I hate Jews or anything, I'm just saying I'm more sexually attracted to very white boys. I think it's because they look like they'd be more fun when they get down and dirty. I like to see someone start out very clean and then get very dirty.

That was the attraction with Cassidy, and I think it all began with my attraction to Jesus. I mean, you just looked at his picture and thought to yourself: wow, it would be so great to see this guy get completely cross-eyed with cum. You could imagine that Jesus would be all embarrassed after sex, and say, "Shit, I have to go home now, I have to feed my cat, and besides, I'm really straight." That's frustrating, but still it's oh so sexy. The other reason I was really attracted to Jesus was because of all the masochism, you know, on the cross and everything. I know it's really twisted, but what can I say? The way he was sort of contorted on the cross — that woman mentioned all this in her play, it turned her on too, not just me — is so sexy. His legs sort of writhing, just enough to cover up his, I'm sure huge, slightly erect dick. And that stomach. Fuck, I think if it wasn't for Jesus on the cross I could have sex with fat guys. The image of that very flat, slightly contorted stomach: his perfect abs, just breathing in a bit with pain… Oh fuck.

Have you ever seen those major nudes that Michelangelo sculpted? It was near the end of his life, and they were sort of unfinished. Bound slaves and stuff. And they were all writhing like they were trying to get out of the stone. Now scholars have studied this stuff like crazy, to figure out if Michelangelo meant not to finish them and it's like, DUH. Michelangelo was a big homo! It's a documented fact, and nothing could be sexier than the image of some beautiful young guy trying to escape from anything with his legs all twisted and his stomach just gasping with pain. In a way, all this makes no sense because, obviously, I have no desire to be crucified. It would be terrible. But I do have these fantasies, like after the major pain was over you'd be on display for all to see and there's nothing you could do about it. Which would be so sexy. This whole fantasy definitely extends into Tarzan fantasies, because Tarzan was always being tied up to some tree and almost burned to a crisp by the natives. (The almost burned part is very important.)

Oh yeah, one more thing, and then I'll get back to Cassidy. I should mention this girl, Laura, who I knew when I was a kid. She was fabulous. She was a ten-year-old dominatrix. She was the first person to help me explore all these masochistic fantasies. You see, Laura, she was southern and had this very cool accent, and she used to invite all the kids from the neighbourhood down to her basement. Then she'd tie us up. And then we'd play slave. It was so fantastic. She'd whip us with something, I can't remember what: it might as well have been a wet noodle, actually. But we could go through all these agonies — "Oh no, don't do that to me, no don't!"— and stuff, and it was great. I just wish someone had filmed it. All these little kids lying around on the floor pretending to be tied up while Laura shouted at them and slapped them with a piece of string. Boy, she must have made some guy really happy (or maybe some girl, who knows, she was kinda butch).

So what I'm trying to explain to you is why I get so obsessed with being guilty. It's been drummed into me with religion and stuff since I was a kid. So when the cops were kind of laying low and not catching the guy who raped Cassidy it was making me very nervous. I mean I didn't do it; but I felt, like I said before, that I could have done it. And then there was Cassidy himself.

Like I said, there was a point when I thought maybe Cassidy had made up the whole assault thing just to get me to pay attention to him. I know it sounds crazy, but he seemed to be sort of following me around. Though it probably had a lot to do with the fact that I refused to see him after the attack.

Yeah, it sounds kind of mean. Even suspicious. But basically I was acting on the advice of the police. They'd actually told me (over one of their smiley lunches) that I should stay away from Cassidy. He was bad news, they said, "an accident waiting to happen." Now I'm not saying they blamed Cassidy. No, like I said before, that wouldn't be right. But they were sort of suggesting that trouble followed Cassidy around. And it's true. For whatever reason. Some people are like that. They always get into trouble. They always seem to be around trouble even if they don't really bring it on themselves, it's just... Well, if my friend Barb, for instance, had read his cards, she would have said that there was something in his moon rising, or not rising or something. Anyway, I thought, "Hey, when the police tell you to stop dating someone, maybe you should stop."

So I stayed away from Cassidy, though that was easier said than done. First of all, we hung out at all the same sleazy old places, bars and bathhouses and backrooms and stuff. And now and then I'd be drunk, and Cassidy would be drunk, and he'd come sidling up to me and look at me with his big eyes, which really were baby blue in the sense that he was such a big sexy baby, and he'd say, "Are you mad at me?" And I'd go, "No." Even though I wanted to give him a big sexy swat, which I knew he'd love, and then he'd say, "Do you hate me?" Now that has to be one of the stupidest questions in the world. I mean, let me give you some advice. If you ever have to walk up to somebody and ask, "Do you hate me?" — well, just don't.

(Actually, "Do you hate me?" isn't the question I hate the most. The one I hate the most would have to be the very gay question, "What are you into?" I know it's not really relevant now, but I have to get it off my back. It's just this question that guys ask you sometimes when they want to pick you up. And it makes me sick. Because first of all, it's kind of like "Do you hate me?" in the sense that, if you have to ask it, you shouldn't. I mean, isn't the whole idea of sex that it's supposed to be spontaneous? Admittedly, I only learned that when I turned gay and started having sex in alleys and bathhouses, but I'm sure there are some straight people who have spontaneous sex too. It just seems to me that the whole point of sex is kind of... suspense. I mean...will he come in my face? Will he come at all? Will he hurt me? Will he suddenly roll over and say: "Oh please fuck me for the first time in my life, please, with your big purple dick?" Stuff like that. So what fun is sex supposed to be when you've already told the guy, "Well, I'm into tit sucking, and could you please do that for approximately five minutes, alternating with mild ball torture. And when my dick is fully erect, frig me for ten minutes while rubbing my big hairy navel every sixth second?" Oh yeah, great, thanks. Sounds like fun. I find it a big problem, actually, because the world is filled with unspontaneous fags who are always asking me, "What are you into?" I usually say "Nothing." Or I just turn away. I mean, I've tried being honest, or at least semi-honest. I guess that's my problem. Maybe, I mean, I could really get rid of these losers if I was honest. Usually I say "I'm kind of a bottom." That means "submissive" in gay talk. But next time when they say, "What are you into?" I think I'll go, "I'm into shit." And they'll probably say, "What particular shit is that?" So I'll go, "Just plain old-fashioned everyday smelly shit. Yours, actually. Eating it." That'll get rid of some these unspontaneous assholes in a millisecond!)

So to get back to Cassidy, he would ask me these manipulative questions and I would say, "No I don't hate you," because I really didn't. Also I just wanted him off my back. I probably shouldn't have talked to him at all because then he'd always say something like, "We had some pretty good times together, didn't we?" And I'd be drunk and I'd look at him and think of my dick in his mouth or his fine fat white ass spread on the toilet and I'd think, "Yeah, we sure did." Of course that was his whole plot, his whole plan. And it was then that I realized he was a stalker.

This guy was just not going to give up. And like all these guys, the fact that I wasn't interested any more just made him want me more. I mean, it was probably partially my fault; I shouldn't have even looked at him in the goddamn bars. But now and then, he was just there, with this "you and me were meant for each other" look in his eyes. And I have to admit, in a way we *were* meant for each other. In bed, anyway. Unfortunately, it's not often you find someone who turns you on that much.

I don't want to give you the wrong idea; basically, I was very good. I never paid any attention to him except now and then to answer his stupid cloying questions because I thought at least that would keep him out of my hair for a while.

So the assault went unsolved and Cassidy kept eyeing me and the police never called. They did come up with one last theory though. One last hare-brained theory: that someone tried to kill Cassidy because they were after me.

Now I know that doesn't make much sense at first, but maybe I haven't *really* explained who I am. I'm supposed to be this important figure in my god-damned gay community. I'm sorry if I sound bitter, but most people in my position are. I mean, I spent years working for gay rights and acting fag parts in plays (most fag actors avoid gay parts like the plague), and do you think anyone in the gay community could give a flying fuck? No, mainly people just resent me. Let's face it: most fags are closeted, especially these days (AIDS did that too), and I've always been really out about my sexuality, and what I like in bed and every-thing, even in interviews. I mean a lot of actors claim they're out, but if they give an interview they *should* mention it. Nobody wants to know you're gay. You, unfortunately, have to force it on people. Or they'll assume you're straight. Also, I've been this big drag queen. I've done it all and then I've admitted it (an unforgivable sin). And so a lot of people resent me. Even other gay people, because they think we gays should be nice and quiet and conservative, and I'm not. I've always been a major shit kicker. (And a major confessor of everything in my gay life. Sometimes I think the whole confessing thing is about all the guilt I carry around, but it just seems I can never confess enough to get it off my back.)

So anyway, the skinny is, I'm a famous fag. And the *Sun*, which is like a very sleazy conservative paper, has been trying to destroy me for years. It is the type of paper that thinks it's cool to print a picture of some stupid broad in a bathing suit next to the front page, and then just to show how fair and progressive they are, print some tiny picture of a dumb bodybuilder, usually some security guard, in black and white, near the back. (It's supposed to be for the women to look at, but it's mainly fags that rush to buy it.) But nobody ever flips to the back of the paper anyway (except horny fags). The stupid shits who read the *Sun* can barely get past the hot chick on page three before they start beating their wife and kids. And the *Sun* hates blacks and immigrants; it's totally fucked. You know the kind of paper. Every town has a rag like it; sometimes it's the only one.

So anyway, there are people from this paper, and even from the gay community, who would probably like to see me dead because I'm such a loudmouth about my sexuality and everything. And this nice policewoman was just trying to help, I guess, suggesting that somebody was trying to get to me through Cassidy.

In my mind it was very unlikely. First of all, Cassidy wasn't even my boyfriend. I just did sleazy things with him and dated him a few times. It wasn't like the whole town knew him as my lover or something. So, I mean, it wouldn't be as if killing the guy would like get me all upset. I hardly knew him; he'd never even seen my apartment. Now this was very hard to explain to the chickies in uniform because they weren't really up on their gay culture and stuff. And as I said before, I don't think they really understood how a guy could get real intimate with another guy and not be his boyfriend. Even though it happens to a lot of fags, like ten times a day.

But the reason I mention this last interview with the cops (the last one before things started to get really messed up) is because I think it might have had something to do with the changes I started to make in my life. In fact, the whole Cassidy assault thing had a lot to do with that. It was kind of a turning point for me, when I'd realized that maybe I'd gone too far with a certain kind of living. That it was time to change.

Hey, I never thought it would happen to me. I mean, I never thought I'd become one of those hypocritical middle-class fags. But isn't there a saying: *you become what you hate most*, or something like that? Well, there are basically two kinds of fags in this world (just like I'm sure there are two kinds of people in this world). There's the total out-and-out sleaze-bags. And then there's the "nice" people. Now, out-and-out sleazebags are not just the whores, drug dealers, drag queens and alcoholics. I'm talking about all the people who are honest. Everyone from those who are proud of being a degenerate to the ones who, at least, don't lie about it. Those who mostly revel in it. Like in the days of Bacchus when all those wild ladies threw their hair down and followed their god into the hills and danced their tits off until the uptight guy (I can't remember his name) came in and killed Bacchus and told them to stop. Like the people who say, "Hey, we're here on this earth to have fun, get drunk and high, and that's what I'm going to do." Now of course all the other people in the world (the hypocrites) have theories about these people. They say they're evil and that they're trying to run from the truth and themselves and real life and their responsibilities. But the way I look at it, it's all a matter of perspective. I mean, who's to say that being stoned isn't (like they said in the sixties) the way to find the essence of all things? I know that isn't a very popular theory right now, and most people say that junkies just end up dead. A lot of them do. But everybody does, right? I mean if you ask me to name one living junkie I'll name one: William Burroughs. Except that he just died, I know. But shit, he lived to be like eighty-three or something. He was doing just fine, thank you. I mean, he killed his wife and everything. Which was not very nice (a homo who kills his wife and it's an *accident*, like we *really* believe that). I'm not condoning his whole life or saying he's a sweet person, but lots of unstoned people kill people too. I'm just saying he lived to be quite an old junkie. And then there's Timothy Leary, another famous sixties guy who was a very stoned person. Yeah, he's also dead, but he was fucked up all his life and still managed to be reasonably articulate. In fact, listen, I'm not recommending getting stoned and drunk and having sex all the time. I'm just saying it's human. And if you try to ignore it you're in for trouble. I mean look at Prohibition. It didn't work (I just saw this documentary on A&E about it), and it's a perfect example of what I'm talking about because even all the religious I-have-to-protect-my-children, sexless-mother types just *had* to come out in favour of drinking when they realized that everybody was going to kill everybody else just to get a drink when it was banned.

Which brings me to coffee. I know this may seem like I'm drifting into Never-Never Land but bear with me. Coffee, to me, today, is just the the biggest symbol of all the hypocrisy in the world. These days, we're seeing the big comeback of the "coffee shop." All the yuppies are going to coffee shops, right? Oh they just love to get up early and have a good run after giving the wife a snuggle, read their copy of the *New York Times* and have a coffee. Hey, it's intellectual and safe, right? Wrong. Coffee is a drug, one of the biggest around. I'm sorry if I'm revealing myself as a real TV watcher here, but CNN is going through one of these phases where they're reporting that coffee is lethal and people should stop drinking it. Well my big question is, what are the big yuppie coffee addicts going to do when their legal little drug is made illegal? I sure as hell don't know. They sure won't march on Starbucks, they're much too sweet and nice to do that. But you get my point here? Even the yuppies have their drug. And if it's not coffee it's something else. So what I'm saying is that everyone has their drug. It might be sex or TV or coke or alcohol or brutality or lying or who knows what. But everybody does something evil and destructive and addictive. (I'm sorry, shopping does *not* count. Shopping just happens to be one of those pseudo- addictions they've been building up on talk shows to make people think they're living out their deepest fantasies, but shopping does not count as an addiction. I'm sorry. Gambling, now *that's* destructive. But not *shopping*.)

So you see what I mean about two kinds of people? There's basically the people who think it's okay to be drugged-out sex freaks, and then there's the people who deny that possibility in themselves and others (mostly in others). They are the hypocrites. They're hell-bent on changing human nature, but it's really impossible. And in the gay community it's just worse, because gay men are so guilty about being gay anyway. All of them; they can't help it. So when gay men get all sanctimonious it's a sad thing to watch. The sanctimonious fags are easy to spot; they're all dog-walkers.

Do you remember that scene in *Midnight Cowboy* with the sad old whore walking her mangy little dog? Well it's the same with so many fags. Why? Well, these fags would never be caught cruising; no, they would never do that. They're oh so faithful to their goddamn lovers, or else they're just "celibate" (oh how I hate that word). But these nice church-going fags, they've sure as hell all got dogs and they've just got to walk them. And they do. Any night in any burg, large or small, city or town or truck stop, the fags will be out walking their dogs. And of course they can't just walk their damn dog in long pants and a long coat and a big ugly floppy hat, can they? No, they've just got to walk the beast in a pair of shorts cut halfway up their arse. Or a short coat, or no shirt at all, or one of those little half shirts, if it's summer, that's cut right above the nipples. (Oh God, how I hate it when they wear those shirts cut right at the nipples — they're ridiculous.)

If I sound bitter, it's because I am. And it's not that I have something against flirtatious clothing. Hey, I love it when honest whores and fags dress to the nines and show their business. I'm talking about hypocrites here. People who dress like that and say they're only walking their dog. But they sure as hell wouldn't be averse to picking up some guy and giving them a swell blowjob while Fido takes a poo, would they? No, they wouldn't. And they do. They do it all the time. Next time you see some hypocrite fag walking a dog just ask him for a blowjob. If he protests and says no, it won't take much to wear the little hypocrite down, I guarantee it.

So how this translates into gay politics is — well, it's abysmal shit. Basically you're either a nice dog-walking church-going fag (hypocrite) or you're a sleazy lousy slut drag queen whore. I've always honestly fallen into the latter category. Until all this shit (and I do mean shit) happened with Cassidy. And then I started to mend my ways.

I know that sounds weird, the idea of me "mending my ways." You can't ask a leopard to change its spots, eh? But I just thought I could change my life a bit. I wasn't going to completely stop drinking and doing drugs and having sex. But I wanted to change my life. I wanted to find true love. I thought that if I did, I could stop thinking about Cassidy and all the violence and especially the shit fantasies.

So I found a very good therapist to help me. This guy was a real winner and I knew he could support me in my new life. You know, people who are looking to change their lives, they don't go to a guru who magically changes everything (despite themselves). No: people subconsciously know what they want to become, and they pick the guru who will take them there. Hell, they practically *make* the guru take them there. What I figured I needed was a nice middle-class uptight fag therapist who could help me become respectable. So I got one. I found someone who would be a bit offended by things I did in my life. This guy had the padded chair and the wooden bookshelves and everything. He was perfect. (At one point he even wrinkled his nose at me and said, "Couldn't you just show some restraint?" And he was supposed to be the non-directional type. Hey, leave it to me to get a non-directional therapist to become directional!)

Later I found out this therapist was a stalker himself. I'm not kidding. This is a great story actually. When I first met him he said, "Oh, you're an actor," and I said, "Yes," and he said, "Maybe you know my actor friend, Liam." And I thought this was very weird. I mean, are therapists supposed to just say, "Do you know my friend so and so?" like we're best buds or something? But he seemed so perfect. He seemed like the perfect nerd to transform me into the middle-class type, so I decided to ignore it. Well, about a year later, after all this Cassidy business was over, I *did* meet his actor friend Liam. Because a friend of mine started dating him. Well, for some crazy reason I mentioned Liam in therapy. Him, and the fact that he was dating my friend. Well my therapist went nuts. He lost all of his middle-class cool and started quivering and sweating. And he stopped the session and told me to go home because he was upset.

Of course this put me in a tizzy, because I could see that my therapist needed a little therapy of his own. Then one night I'm out for a drink with Liam and the friend he's dating, and Liam's a little drunk and he turns to me and says, "Hey, do you think you could get your goddamn therapist to stop stalking me? Ever since you told him I was sleeping with David he's been on my case. He phones me ten times a day." Can you believe it? So it ended up that my nice, middle class therapist, the guy with books on the wall who was always recommending restraint, was actually stalking this stupid actor kid. He was probably sucking his feet or something. Foot sucking, that has to be the one thing people are the most guilty about in the whole world. Yeah, I bet he was a foot sucker, my therapist. I bet he used to get down on the floor, take off his little doctor spectacles, and bury his nose in Liam's big hairy feet. And during this time I still just thought he was a very good therapist. I mean, when you're having problems with someone stalking you, who better to help you out than a stalker therapist? And when you're trying to stop having scat fantasies, who better to talk you out of them than a closet foot fetishist? I mean *really*, eh?

Now I know you're probably thinking that this is all completely crazy; that in fact I was completely crazy to think I could change. I mean, after telling you about being a drag queen and being a slut and watching Cassidy take a shit on the couch, how could I ever imagine being respectable? But I did. I wanted to change. I wanted Cassidy to stop following me. I was very serious about the therapist and everything at the time. And I wanted to stop talking to Cassidy. I wanted the police to stop calling me because... well, here's the gist of it: I figured I was guilty (duh!) and I figured that if I could just stop doing all the bad things I did, then the guilt would be gone. *Presto change-o.* You wouldn't be able to read it on me or smell it on me. Cassidy and the police would forget about me because I wouldn't have a whiff of sin or desire about me anywhere.

And I thought, hey, I've just got to find a nice middle-class boy who looks like Cassidy (and hence, a little like Jesus) and fall in love. And the boy has to be into nice clean sex, and I'll stay home most of the time, and never go to bars or the baths again. And I won't be haunted anymore.

That was my plan.

So it was almost like fate (or maybe I was already giving off nice pretty smells or something... I sure started washing my asshole three times a day) that I would meet Roger.

Now don't get me wrong. Roger was no hypocrite, either. Roger was perfect. Well, I can't really say he wasn't a hypocrite. That would be a lie. But he seemed like he was the most unhypocritical person I'd ever met. I guess he would fall into what I would call a third category of people. He was one of the few who just don't have many strange desires. There are people like that. Now I don't think there are many people who, lets say, have no strange desires at all. But I think there are some people, like Roger, who don't have a lot of them. Like Roger's strange desire was simply that he liked to get fucked. And that's not so strange at all. Not in the gay community.

So Roger allowed himself to get fucked. And he allowed himself a little drink now and then. And he was like a really nice guy. Except he was a little bit middle-class. Which I'll explain later. But basically he was someone who was neither an addict or a hypocrite. And that's really hard to find.

I met Roger at this gay dance. Yeah, it was actually a gay dance at some hot and trendy straight bar. And I remember he was standing on the stairs, and I was running down to take a piss because I was so drunk, and Roger was a little drunk (he never got very drunk, ever), and he grabbed me as I was running down the stairs and said, "Hi, big guy" (which was very sweet). Anyone who refers affectionately to my triple-X magnitude always gets my vote. And he was kind of slight. Littler than me. Which is a major turn-on. And he told me that he had always wanted to kiss me.

Just like that, he said it. Oh yeah, first he told me what a great shirt I was wearing. Then he said he'd always wanted to kiss me. And, well, what could I do? I kissed him.

It was on the stairs, so it was extra great. There's a great short story by James Joyce (bet you thought I never read a book in my life) called — I can't remember what it's called, but it's all about a woman standing on a stair, and she hears a violin playing or something and she gets all sad. I think it's called "Distant Music." Anyway, whenever anyone does anything romantic to me on the stairs it reminds me of that. And when I kissed Roger on the stairs it was great.

Then he ran off to his friends, and I ran off to mine. And of course we gossiped about each other. That's what faggots do. It's lethal. I think we all learned it from our goddamned mothers. Have a nice chat or a kiss or a fuck or whatever, and then we run off to our girlfriends. "Oh you'll never guess…" etc. I told everyone about Roger and our stupid kiss. It was a big thing for me. After the incredible little whore episode with Cassidy and the police it was like being fucking reborn — all from Roger's chaste little kiss on the stairs.

Except it wasn't that chaste. I mean it was all very clear. I held him and he held me — but mainly I held him, because he had this tiny waist (he really was slender, like a boy) and I pulled him to me, and when that happens, of course, so much is said. (That is ultimately what I don't get about straight people. I mean it's always the same. Right? The guy always grabs the girl and hugs her and fucks her or rapes her and the woman is, like, reluctant or she yells or she gives in. Now I'm not saying *all* straight people have sex like that all the time — whenever they don't it must be great — but most of the time they do. The roles are so goddamn strict. *He's a big male, he's going to fuck me; I know that, because I'm a girl.* Well I'm a big male, but sometimes I like to suck cock. Now in this particular instance, when I put my arm around this slender boy on the stairway, I could tell he wanted to get his ass ploughed good. And that was a pleasant little message, but a surprise.)

So anyway, I ran up and told my friends, and later they just *had* to meet him. I had two particularly noxious theatre friends at the time: Peter and Anya. Peter was like the talk of the town, a semi-ugly fag from the West Coast who was a performance artist and very pretentious, but suddenly everybody wanted to fuck him. Anya was this incredibly nutty performance artist who everybody thought was a sex change though no one was really sure. I have this other friend (who was quite an unassuming transexual) who said that people who have sex changes shouldn't talk about it, they should just shut up. I know that sounds really horrible and oppressive but I know what she means. I think some fags should just shut up too. (Not me of course!) This couple was so pretentious they were just about ready to move to Soho (New York or London take your pick). He was doing this semi-drag (I hate semi-drag — either put on a dress or don't, okay?) poetry theatre piece that didn't contain any sentences, only words. He was a damn good semi-drag queen, though. She played the violin and showed her new breasts and talked about how oppressive it was having a penis. [Except I think she still had one. Isn't that just too irritating? I know so many sex changes that go on and on about how wonderful it is to be a woman and they've still got their dicks. And the reason they keep it a secret, of course, is the same old thing: hypocrisy. No one wants to admit they're sleeping with a hermaphrodite (the ultimate perversion), so these so-called sex changes (who are really women with dicks) get laid like crazy. And nobody knows. Well you heard it here first. In fact, chicks with dicks are a very big thing. And no one talks about it (except in the "personal" columns of some straight mags). I mean, a lot of men who pick up hookers are actually picking up chicks with dicks when they cruise around in their cars. The guys are supposedly so "butch" and "horny" that it doesn't matter to them. A hole is a hole. They don't care if it's a guy with a penis sucking them off, as long as it's in a dress. But in fact some of these chicks with dicks do better business than the all-female hookers. They're really in demand. If you try and figure that one out, I think you'll come to some pretty kinky conclusions.] So anyway, I run back to these two incredibly pretentious friends all excited about Roger: me already feeling Roger is like the start of my new life.

I know it might sound contradictory, that I could get so romantic all of a sudden; but that's just my nature. I can't explain it. I am a total sexpig, but then, I'm also totally capable of giving it up when the right guy comes along. Well, hey, I never actually have "given it all up." But I've given up a lot. I mean, I've stayed home three or four nights a week and seriously cut down on the drinking and fucking and everything because some cute boy was waving his ass at me. And this was what I saw as a possibility with Roger. Now most guys I feel this way about just turn out to be silly boys. So I ran back and told pretentious friends number one and two and they were like completely unimpressed. "Oh yeah, who did you kiss, who?" I pointed him out and Peter was so blasé: he just got that bored look that says, "Oh yeah, I guess you *would* find someone like him attractive." And Anya immediately said that she had to go over and check him out. I couldn't stop her because she was drunk, and even though she was low-key and sort of self-effacing, she was also persistent.

So she runs over to Roger and introduces herself and starts probing him. I'm watching her and it's making me very nervous. I know she wouldn't reveal that she's my friend or anything, only it's pretty obvious that she is because I've been standing with her. But I like the way Roger carries himself when he talks with her. Sort of awkwardly. Like he has no idea that he's cute. That's very appealing. (It's sensible to date a guy like that. It's always a great idea to get a boyfriend who doesn't really know he's cute. He's much more faithful to you, and you get points for building up his self-esteem whenever you tell him how cute he is.) So Anya runs back and makes some sort of mystical sign of disapproval.

"No" she goes, "no no no no." And I go, "Why?" And she goes, "His energy is very bad, very negative. He's a climber. He's definitely a climber." Now this refers to my social and theatrical status. Peter nods his head like he just knew this guy was horrible without even looking at him again. And I'm like thinking, "*Oh, right.* You, Anya, and you, Peter, are performance artists, for Christsakes. In an era when even real performance artists have decided that the fucking art form is dead. You two are the climbingest fucking people in the world. You'd climb onto any art form you thought had potential."

(I mean Peter won't ever sleep with anybody unless they're successful or they have huge, evident potential. Once I went out to dinner with Peter and... well, first of all, Peter is a lethally charming person. Have you ever met one of those? He is like so incredibly entertaining he could charm the pants off of anyone. And he's not even hot. But boy can he talk; he's the type of guy who can make you feel like you are the centre of the fucking universe. And he can make you believe you're funny. Because he is. Himself. He's very funny, he's a good mimic, very nasty and catty and just a scream. So when you're with him you think you're a scream, and you think you're in love with him, and you think he's in love with you. I have so many friends who have fallen in love with Peter and Peter just fucks them and drops them, mainly because they're not successful enough. I haven't fallen for him mainly because he's a bit pudgy, but also because he has this kind of weird straight semi-grey hair all over his body which I find totally disgusting. Some people think it's all manly and daddylike but it just reminds me of some ugly wet dog. Even when he's dry. So anyway, when we were out having dinner this waiter said that Peter looked just like Phil Collins and the waiter — I have to admit he was really cute — for some strange reason thought that Phil Collins was attractive. I personally hate it, when someone tells you that you look like someone totally ugly and then they say, "Oh don't worry, I think he's attractive," because I'm like, who cares? I don't want to look like Orson Welles! People always always say I look like Orson Welles; it drives me crazy. They say, "You look like Orson Welles when he was young and attractive." And that's supposed to make a difference? I don't want to look like Orson Welles. Even if he did marry Rita Hayworth, he was too fat! I want to look like, I don't know... James Dean or something. Not Orson Welles. Young or old, fat or not so fat. But anyway, this guy thought Peter looked like Phil Collins and told him so, and I told Peter to fuck him. I mean, the waiter was really cute and — oh I forgot. The guy was a busboy. He wasn't even a waiter. He was a busboy, so that was the crux of the whole thing, right? I said, "You've got to fuck him Peter, he's cute." And Peter just looked at me and said, "Jack, he's a busboy," with ultimate disgust. So that was when I decided that Peter and I were completely different. Like, I could fuck any cute busboy anywhere. I couldn't care less what anybody does for a living. Besides, sometimes very smart people have very stupid jobs. Some of the most profound people I have ever met are cab drivers.)

So anyway, the fact that Peter and Anya didn't like Roger and thought he was a climber was kind of a recommendation in my books.

(Oh, I just have to tell you one more thing about

Peter and Anya: it was a little while after all this that they invited me over to their new third-floor-of-an-old-house apartment that they had just moved into together. And it was such a scream: they decided they were going to have a sort of sexless marriage and create performance art in their new space — it had a huge deck for "summer performances." And they made this fabulous dinner, and we exchanged presents — it was around Christmas — and it was snowing outside and all cozy. And Anya made me these little bouquets of dead wildflowers that were guaranteed to chase away bad spirits — let me tell you, they didn't work. After dinner they were going to do a performance, or something, which I find completely disgusting. Like, is this your home, or a theatre? I just find all the avant-garde "my home is a theatre" stuff beyond stupid. But anyway they never got to the performance because they started having a huge fight, which was kind of a performance in itself. In fact they may have intended that. Anyway, Anya told Peter that he had deep-seated fears about sex changes. And Peter told Anya that she was homophobic. So they decided they couldn't live together and Anya ran out into the snow to freeze to death. We could see her through the window, Peter and I, and it really was very beautiful. She sat in the snow shivering for hours. And then Peter started to take pictures of her with his camera and the whole thing became a performance-art piece about their argument. At that point I had to go. I mean, I only came over for dinner.)

So now that you have a picture of Peter and Anya, you can see why their whole negative opinion just spurred me on about Roger. So I went over to talk to him. He was a really nice guy, I could tell that right away. He had dyed-blond hair, which I love, and he was part Inuit, which I love too. He was doing his Masters degree in some sort of metaphysics. This I found very interesting, because he was into stuff about life and death that I couldn't even fathom. My God, Roger was smart. He always used to ask me to read his papers and I could never understand them. But the main thing I was interested in about him was his hair distribution. He was part Inuit and hair distribution is very related to race (as well as age) so I just wanted to know: like, how much hair does he have — and where?

So there was a sexual fascination from the start. And then Roger started talking to me about my being a drag queen, and he wasn't sure if he was comfortable with drag queens, so we got into some really interesting talks about gender and drag and feminism and political correctness. (I bet you wouldn't believe that I could talk about that shit, but I can. I am very strange that way. Believe it or not I am quite the intellectual. It's just that most people I know who are smart are such assholes: much too proud of it. So I hide it and refuse to talk as if I have a brain in my head. But with a cute boy with interesting hair distribution who likes big guys I can suddenly become an expert on Lacan. *The gaze... the gaze...* oh dear.)

So I could tell that Roger was into me, very much, sexually, but a little bit scared of the fact that I was such an out-there, sexual, guy. I get this a lot. My technique is to get them into bed and fuck them really good and then convince them that I'm an okay guy after their mind is already fogged up by sex.

And basically it worked that night. I took Roger home and played him the Cowboy Junkies' *Trinity Sessions*, which is something I save only for really beautiful guys that I want to see again. And he had just the right amount of hair on his legs: it stopped right before his ass. And he loved to get fucked by my big cock. I didn't tell him, because it would have upset him, but I was having major coach-and-student fantasies while I was fucking him. Maybe it was because Roger was a student or something, but I was just really riffing on fantasies like the student comes in to talk to the coach about some problems he's having with his game or something, and the coach just rims the kid, then whips it out and gets down and fucks him. So everything was peachy-keen in that department.

And we got up the next day and I made him breakfast and everything. It was really very idyllic. Pretty soon we were dating. I knew Roger was looking for a lover (he was the lover type), and I knew I was the one. And it seemed to me that we were going to have this great relationship.

So I went to my yuppie (future stalker) therapist and said, "Hey, I've met Roger and he's a really nice boy and we have normal I-fuck-you-up-the-ass-with-a-condom-and-withdraw-just-before-I-come sex, and he's smart and together, and I think I'm really changing my life." My therapist just nodded his head (as I said, he was non-directional) and asked me, "So how do you *feel*?"

I felt great. I really did think I was changing. Roger and I would go to lots of plays about the Inuit. There were always plays about the Inuit playing in town at the time (it was a big theatre rage) and all the straight white old ladies would go and see the plays. The quality of the plays was varied. I mean, the quality didn't matter to these old theatre ladies, and they were the ones with the big bucks for tickets. Now I'm not saying Inuit theatre is bad. (And I can understand how important it is to fight that whole Eskimo thing.

Because, you know, it's the same thing as gay theatre. I mean, I get a lot of flack from uptight gay men for playing drag queens in gay plays. It's like if you're an "oppressed people," then sometimes you get uptight seeing images of yourself oppressed. But my view of all this is: so what if everyone thinks drag queens are disgusting? They aren't. So even if straight people think we shouldn't act like drag queens, there's no point in sucking up to straight people. And I think the same thing applies to the Inuit and Eskimos. I mean the whole concept of Eskimo is sort of like the concept of drag queen. They dress in a way that is funny to the general public, for instance. And a lot of Inuit people don't want to be seen as Eskimos. But on the other hand, there's lots of things about being an Eskimo that are part of the Inuit experience, not just a white version of it, if you know what I mean. So it was interesting for me, as a gay drag queen performer, to look at the way the Inuit dealt with Eskimos.) And some of the Inuit theatre was pretty good, actually. But when it comes to these old theatre ladies, I have to say that Inuit theatre can get away with murder. I mean, basically, it's reverse racism, right? Because it's Inuit work, the Inuit are allowed to get naked and talk dirty, right? Basically, because they're not white people they're "exotic," with a different culture. All the plays about Inuit people can be really sexual and shocking, but all the rich old ladies who go and see the plays aren't shocked because they can just smile at each other and say, "Oh the Inuit are just like that. It's part of their culture." I swear I've seen old ladies do that; I have. (And equally kinky or outright queer stuff in gay plays usually scandalizes the same people because it's *white* sexual-cultural stuff.) I discussed this with Roger and we had a fight about it. But at least we were relating. We had a good time at all the Inuit plays because Roger could identify with a lot of the issues. One of the plays was about being caught between white society and Inuit society, which was perfect for Roger because he sort of was too, because he was really half-Inuit.

Roger was always worried about whether I found him boring. I never did. Ever.

The best thing about Roger was that he would laugh in bed. Have you ever laughed in bed, I mean while you're having sex? I mean just flip between serious fucking and kidding? I find that very important.

So it was getting pretty serious, we were seeing each other three or four times a week, and then we started introducing each other to our friends. And that's when the trouble sort of started.

It was no problem with my friends. I introduced Roger to Barb right off and she was very impressed with him. Barb is very frank. Right at dinner she leaned over the table and said, "He's not stupid like your other boyfriends." I think it surprised Roger, but he obviously sort of liked it. Barb entertained us with all her adventures with men. She had been seeing this younger guy (she liked younger guys; she was sort of a gay man) who started out French and turned out to be Portuguese. The guy was a major liar. I met him once. He was supposed to be an exchange student and the place he was supposed to live in fell through, so he met Barb at a party and she said she had a room (her painting studio had a bed in it) and he could sleep there for a while. Of course they said he fucking, and she asked him to pay rent — he would pay it, once he got his first *drugstore.* was an apprentice pharmacist wor*ker to train* (Apparently the drugstores her in than the ones in Paris!) So Alphonse (that's what she thought his name was) slept with her, fucked her, didn't pay rent, and disappeared all day to apprentice at the drugstore. Well, next thing you know he disappears for two days in a row. So Barb went to look for him and found out he didn't even work at the drugstore he was supposed to work at. When he finally came home she found out that he wasn't even French. He was Portuguese. (I can't remember how she found out, but I think she really felt gypped. I mean, I've got nothing against Portuguese people; they can be very sexy and romantic too. And the guys have great hair distribution. Very hairy legs and thighs and that's all you need. But you know, Portuguese and French are different. And the whole Paris thing, you know romance, the Eiffel Tower, it's just different than sun and oranges. I mean, as I was saying, nothing against Portuguese guys — who tend to be more uncut even than French and also have huge wangers — but, you know, it's like ordering an ice-cream bar and you've got your heart set on a Mudbar and you end up with a Neapolitan. I mean, you're thinking about nuts and chocolate and you end up with strawberry. This happened to me the other day, actually. You just go, "Ew." Even though strawberry is fine when you're actually expecting it. Same thing with Portuguese when you expect French. Still, Barb was very funny alking about it.) So anyway, she kicked him out, but still fucked him now and then. She said that his had "ruined her for other men." I loved that fu Roger thought Barb was outrageous and talke were perfectly in love. Then Roger started Dut Denton.

impot was obvious that Denton was very oger. He had mentioned him a couple of times: "Oh my friend Denton…" "Oh you have to meet Denton." And the very common, "And Denton says…" Always quoting him. And they were never lovers. Denton was just a friend. An older man friend. Hmmm.

It didn't take me long to figure out that Denton was in love with Roger. That's the way it works with these older man/young man yuppie things.

Let me explain the way the whole hypocritical thing works: in the gay world, when you get older, life becomes incredibly contradictory. On the one hand it's great because there's this whole "bear" scene, which is like the world of the old, fat, hairy fags. They call themselves bears: they have a magazine and everything. It's really quite great. I mean, in my opinion it all started with AIDS. Before AIDS there was this incredible thin chic thing going on, where you just had to be thin. And then after AIDS happened being thin was like not such a great turn-on because that could mean you were sick. So big guys became "in" again. And then they began to form clubs and go for swims and, basically, the whole bear scene is for bigger older guys and the men who love them. One of my friends who is totally into bears — actually he'll only sleep with guys who are short and fat and look like you could order a pizza from them; he is obsessed with these little guys who are always named Joe or Frank — told me, "Hey I was into *bears* when it wasn't in fashion and they were just called *fat*." (He was very pleased that he got to the bear fetish before it was a fad.) Now, this may be true, but I say, what does it matter whether they call them *fat* or *bears* as long as they get sex like everybody else, and love too, if they want it?

So, back to older gay men and the younger ones. In

the gay world, if you're into the bar scene then you definitely know about this whole bear thing. And if you start to get old and fat and you find it traumatic you can go to the bear bars and the bear parties and stuff. I went to this great thing once called the *Teddy Bear's Picnic* and they had a lot of fat hairy old guys just standing around the pool drinking at this bathhouse. It was really great. After one of these parties you could, like, start to feel inadequate if you didn't have a big round belly and some grey in your beard. It was quite a lot of fun. They were throwing little guys into the water. And the big fat bear guys were jumping and whenever they felt like it they would do like a cannonball jump and spill water everywhere, which I thought was fantastic because usually when you do that in a public pool, and you're big, everyone laughs like when some kid drops their tray at the cafeteria, and the fat person feels embarrassed for splashing and making waves. But not at the bear party. I mean some of these guys were so fat and old they had trouble climbing out of the pool. But they were happy. You know what I mean?

I shouldn't let this whole part of our chat end without debunking the whole gay youth and beauty myth. I mean, everybody thinks fags are so into youth and beauty. Give me a break. As if our whole culture isn't. I turned on *Sally Jesse Raphael* the other day and they had this show about a 680-pound woman — "I'm 12 Years Old and I Take Care of My 680-pound Mother" — and it was a great show. I mean, you know the talk shows are doing their job when they make you feel really good about your own life, right? That's their purpose. And watching this huge woman who could barely get out of her chair ordering her twelve-year-old daughter around and forcing her to make more Kraft Dinner, really made me feel like my life, scat or no scat, Cassidy or no Cassidy, was really great. Really first rate. But I couldn't believe it. On this show about fat people they actually had commercials for weight-loss techniques. It was like the whole thing, content and commercials, was completely centred around weight loss. Have you noticed that all the big TV hostwomen are either overweight, or gaining and losing weight all the time? Like Oprah? So don't tell me that all of America is not obsessed with the beauty myth, and with weight loss and gain. And don't tell me gay men are extra special in this department; because they're not.

I should probably tell you about the whole thing about me and weight because I've kind of hinted at it. I'm no Twiggy. I weigh in at 230 easy, and I'm a tall guy. But I've got a belly. I'll always have a belly. That's the way God made me, and I'm proud of it. And I've learned that, in the gay community, the opposite of the youth and beauty thing is actually true. I mean, I have had sex with guys who actually fantasized about my belly, or my weight, or both. A couple of the guys I've fucked would ask me to lie on them. Then they would say stuff like, "Put your whole weight on me." I've had guys who, after they've sort of shyly blown me — ever had a shy blowjob? They're great — actually ask me, "How much do you weigh?" Really horny-like. Well, at first I wouldn't tell them. Because it's a long story. Basically, I was a fat kid and girls used to steal my briefcase and taunt me, and it's just the whole long, maudlin fat kid story. So at first when these guys would ask me how much I weighed I would be really neurotic and not tell them. But after a while I realized that if I told them how much I weighed they might just start wanking again. So then it became a turn-on. I mean, I have been in bars, displaying my belly and all, and guys have just come up to me and asked: "How much do you weigh?" And I often go "Two hundred and forty pounds." Like, I even *add* ten pounds now and then, just for good measure. And the guys will go away shaking their head, like, amazed. "You're some big boy!" they sometimes say. So that should shut everybody up about the whole beauty thing in the gay community. I mean, I'm sure it was true in ancient Greece. But could we forget ancient Greece, like, for a fucking millisecond? I mean, I'm not saying that gay porn isn't totally about muscle guys with huge wieners. I know how hard it is to find bear porn, I've tried. But basically, sex is democratic. That's the great thing about sex, it's like Walt Whitman must have invented it or something. It's true that almost anything, including stumps and deformities, is sexually attractive to somebody. And the gay world being so sexual just makes things more democratic still.

So, anyway, in contrast to this, there's this whole other gay culture around age, which is the much more publicized one because it's sexless and people are usually afraid to look at things sexually. So in this gay cultural model the older gay man doesn't go to bars or anything, he usually has a garden and a nice house and money (usually he's old enough to collect all that) and he just sits around and pines for younger men. Sometimes he has a boyfriend, but even if he does he still pines. And usually the pining revolves around the concept of "Aren't they young and frisky? And don't they have an intense sexual scene? I, however, am older and wiser and beyond that. I couldn't imagine running around in short shorts. I am much too dignified. So I will tend my garden and hug my lover and long for days gone by. It will be sad and a little lonely and not much fun, but that's what it means to be old."

Now I may have gone overboard here a bit, especially when I was describing the gay hypocrites (though these sad old guys are definitely a subset of this group I was describing). Like, I'm perfectly aware that there are probably some old guys who don't go to either bear pool parties or sit around and pine for younger men, because they're perfectly happy being old. There must be some who don't fit into either category. But I think that most gay men fall into one of the two categories. At least, as far as I can see.

And the way these two categories are *so* separate, you'd think that they existed on different planets. Do you think you could get one of those sad old parsley-planting whiny fags into a leather bar in shorts and a harness? No way, he'd rather be dead. These guys just sort of look at each other across the street and go, "There's *that* kind of fag."

Which brings me back to Denton and Roger. Now Denton was not *quite* an old fag. He was only barely fifty. And he looked much younger. He actually had lots of dyed black hair, and it was wavy and gorgeous. And he was very slight, which looked wonderful on him. I mean, he would have to get hit by a truck before he actually aged. Now Denton was the exact opposite of a bear. It wasn't his fault, because physically he could never be a bear. No, I take that back. Denton being little and hairless wasn't necessarily what stopped him. I mean, I have gone to leather bars and seen little hairless guys standing in the corner all leathered up and smoking cigars who managed to convince everyone they were big bear daddies just by smelling up the place with a robusto and carrying a whip. So even Denton could have been a kind of bear. But he definitely did not want to be.

No, Denton was a very persnickety sort. I was never quite sure what he did for a living, but it had something to do with "the arts." He was always very much up on "the arts." His apartment was very lovely, with original works by various painters, and each room was painted a different colour. And he had these fabulous coffee table art books that were limited editions and everything. I mean, Denton had the kind of apartment where if you turned around too fast you might break something priceless. Which always made me wonder what would happen if he ever brought home a trick. I mean what do these fancy fags do about street trade when they bring them home? Do they hide the silver?

And what if the kid is into scat?

Actually, I think that's the point. I don't think Denton ever tricked. I think he just collected intelligent and interesting young men. And Roger was one of them. Denton would find these interesting young men at art openings and such. And there would always be a gaggle around him, and now and then he would take one as a lover. These relationships usually lasted for a couple of years and then the kid would grow up and realize that Denton was shallow and pretentious.

Then it was bye-bye Denton.

The reason I say Denton was pretentious was because he *knew* people. I mean, he knew somebody who had slept with somebody who had slept with Noel Coward. He even told me that this guy he used to know (he's dead now, not AIDS, he just got old!) once was staying over at old Noel's place and that Noel used to call Marlene Dietrich in Paris or wherever the hell she was, and have her sing a nice little song over the phone just 'cause he liked her voice.

Now that kind of anecdote would have impressed me if it had come from anybody but Denton. I don't know what it was, exactly, maybe the fact that he was so *proud* of having known all these famous people. Or maybe it was just the fact that Denton was so peppy (not preppy — he was that too — but peppy).

I think that's it, actually. Denton was terminally peppy. I don't know if you've ever met a terminally peppy person. (Some of them are straight — a lot of them are straight women, in fact.) But terminally peppy people always make me tired. When a terminally peppy person comes over to talk to me I just start yawning. They make me want to burp and fart and, yes, shit. Because these peppy people are usually very clean. Almost antiseptic.

And the peppy thing was somehow all linked with walking on his toes. Denton would sort of bounce around on his toes. Since he was a such a little guy I guess he thought it was cute. It probably was cute — when he was twenty and his ass had some lift. But now you just knew he had a saggy ass underneath those white pants of his, so carefully pleated, and the bounce was just annoying. And he always had an anecdote and something to say, and he was always ready to show you his latest goddamn art acquisition. And he was always full of energy and ready to like suddenly say, "Let's go skiing!" or "Let's play tennis!" or something. You know, something where you have to wear white and put a little bit of that horrible skin protection stuff on your nose. No, Denton could never, of course, get a tan. He burned. Unlike me. I like to get completely black. I mean, once I got so tanned that I brought this guy home with me and he woke up in the morning and he started screaming (he was a racist), "Oh my God, I've gone to bed with a black man! Oh my God!"

He left. Good riddance, I say; I always have a hard time getting a hard-on when I sleep with racists. That is, if I find out they're racists before we have sex.

I know I'm painting this horrible picture of Denton, but he really, like, basically, caused all this trouble between Roger and me. I'm actually ready to go on record to say that he drove me to murder: if I did, that is, actually murder someone. So if I seem to be going overboard about Denton it's because I have my reasons.

Now the fact that Roger was friends with this guy was definitely something I found as terminally depressing as Denton's general pep. When I first met Denton, at some goddamn art opening or something, it was all I could do to keep from asking Roger, "Who was that creep?" But I could see that Roger really liked him so I shut up. I mean, if you're starting a relationship with someone you really have to put up with things. Like, you have to accept a wart on their navel or something. I figured Denton was Roger's wart. After all, Roger was only twenty-five and Denton could be very impressive to someone who didn't have a lot of experience. And Roger was a kind of cultural sociologist, not an artist. That's another thing I liked about him. I mean, I like to sleep with people who are either completely stupid (like Cassidy), or guys who are into something so completely out of my league like "Metaphoric Aspects of Integers" that I can't judge them too much. Anyway, Denton was the type of arty person who just loved everything trendy. His tastes were very sweeping. Yeah, sure, I tried to tell Roger the truth about Denton in my own little way. Like I'd say to him, "Roger, did you notice that Denton has never heard of Frank O'Hara?" To me, this was a dead give-away. I mean, you're supposed to be a gay arty person and you've never heard of the most fabulous gay poet who ever lived? No, Denton was into Christopher Isherwood and stuff, which is fine. I'm not knocking Isherwood. They made *Cabaret* out of his book and everything, and he married some guy thirty years younger than him and they lived happily ever after for their whole lives. So I'm not knocking old Christopher Isherwood. But he's the only gay writer that someone like Denton would ever have heard of. But this conversation never really went anywhere. Although I did get to read Roger some Frank O'Hara poems in bed. (It was luscious, I fucked him good afterwards.) But it's like, you know how it is, Roger began to get an inkling that I didn't like Denton. And then I knew it might become an "issue" — so I just dropped hating him.

But what began to get really annoying was that Roger started to make it very clear that it was important that Denton liked me. And this started to make me really mad.

He was very shy about it at first, because Roger's a nice guy. And at least he was very honest. He'd say things like, "You know Denton is one of my best friends." When I asked him why, he went on and on about how Denton had helped him when he had been going out with this creepy abusive guy. I don't mean really abusive. Roger would never go out with some-one who actually beat him up or anything: he wasn't perverted enough for shit like that. But Roger had been dating some guy who was a terminal liar and who went to the bathhouse all the time and didn't tell him. And Roger had been totally into this guy's big uncut cock, so he put up with the lies for a long time. (Roger was a bit of a size queen, which didn't bother me at all; I took it as a compliment.) Now when it came to me and the sleaze world, I made it very clear to Roger that I was going to give it up. And I really was going to. I was trying. I only went to the baths like once every two weeks when I was with him, and I completely knocked out the parks and toilets (which was tough for me because, as you might have guessed, I *loved* the toilets: I did hang out at the toilets in the bathhouse, which was sort of a compromise, but when you're dealing with an addiction you have to start slow). But I mean I was very honest with Roger about the fact that I was trying to change my life. I told him that I had to go slowly, and he knew I went cruising now and then, and he didn't ask me about it. I promised I could stop completely after six months. But as you'll see, we never got to six months.

Anyway, Roger had been going out with this liar: which is the worst thing in the world. I mean, I think there's nothing in the world as bad as having someone lie to you. And Roger was being fooled by this guy for about six months. It got to the point where people were coming up to him in bars and saying, "You'll never guess where I saw Mike." Well, Roger did the ultimate gay thing. (Everybody goes through this at one time or another.) He decided to go to the baths himself on the night Mike always went to the bathhouse (according to the friends who ratted on Mike). Actually, it was early evening. That's the time, in fact, to catch all the guys with lovers and wives. Early evenings at the baths or parks or toilets. I mean these married types can always tell spousey that they had to stay late at the office or some other crap. If you go to the sleazy places late at night that's when you meet the really nice honest people. Not the liars.

Anyway, Roger went to the bathhouse at cocktail time, and of course he saw Mike there, and he almost hit him. He *should* have hit him. But Roger's too nice a guy, so he left crying. And of course he called Denton and spent the night at Denton's house, and Denton comforted him. I guess you can get a lot of comfort from bad art.

I never asked if they slept together. Even though I imagined the scenario. I imagined Denton tiptoeing into Roger's little room (Denton has a spare bedroom that he fixes up very seriously with trendy art to suit whatever boy has fallen for him for that year), and just, you know, giving Roger a chaste kiss or something. (Maybe even hugging him for awhile, which makes me nauseous.) But to imagine Denton's white little body pressed against Roger's... No, sorry. Even if it happened I refuse to imagine it.

So when someone has had this kind of epiphany where they suddenly realize that their life is fucked and they have to break up with a liar, and they get comforted all night and everything, well then I guess this person, like, becomes a lifelong friend. I understand how it happened. I just wish it hadn't happened with a peppy creep like Denton.

So, anyway, Roger was harping on how he wanted Denton and me to get to know each other. (Which means he wanted Denton to approve of me: I mean, I'm sure he probably wanted me to approve of Denton too, but I was being so nice about it — because I loved him — that he probably wasn't half as worried about my feelings, which, looking back on it, made things unequal.) So of course I had to give in and go to the goddamn dinner.

Oh God how I dreaded it. Of course it was one of those things that had to be talked about and prepared for over and over again. And I was doing everything in my power to make it really clear that I had no bad feelings about Denton, which I'm sure was a stupid thing to do. But I knew if I said a bad thing about Denton it would just start this huge rift between Roger and me, which of course I didn't want. And to tell you the truth, I really didn't know how horrible Denton was until that dinner. Before that, he was just peppy and a representation of the kind of fag I tend to dislike.

Also, I have to admit, at that time I considered the whole thing a kind of test for myself. I mean, I knew that if Roger and I were going to become "lovers" then we'd probably have to attend these kinds of goddamn dinner parties once or twice a month. (It's basically part of being a fag with a lover, unless you want to hide under a rock.) And so I thought that maybe if I could get used to it, with this horrible fag who had actually probably been in a bed with Roger (ugh!), then I could get used to anything. It was a trial by fire sort of scene.

I can't really tell you how horrible the whole affair was. But of course I'll try. Naturally we had to make sure to buy wine and everything, and I went out and bought Piat d'Or. Now, I'm sorry but I thought Piat D'Or was a perfectly respectable wine. I suppose the big problem with it, in Roger's view, was it was advertised on TV. But I always really liked those commercials where the woman sort of purrs Piat D'Or with this sexy voice. And it just sounded great and I had tried it, and it was sort of fruity (how appropriate), which was okay for me because I don't really like dry wine. But apparently one doesn't bring TV wine to a dinner party. And this I found out like half an hour before we went. Roger was over at my place and we were going through one of my fashion crises. I know, I haven't told you about them. Well, I always have a fashion crisis whenever I have to go someplace that I'm not used to going. I mean, I'm used to dressing for the bars, which means basically wearing nothing; I'm very into cut off shirts and T-shirts and see-through shirts that show my tattoos. And I like to wear tight pants. This was a summer dinner, and I am also into wearing shorts that are cut up to the asshole. (Remember, I told you I have nothing against clothes like this if you're openly sluttish. Of course, I knew this posed another problem: if I was less openly sluttish, could I still dress this way? Hmmm.) But I knew, anyway, that none of my normal apparel was right for dinner with Denton. I do actually have some normal shirts, and I was trying them on for Roger, and Roger was very good-naturedly telling me which was the best and also kidding me about the way I make funny faces in the mirror when I'm trying on clothes. That's another stupid thing I do and it became a sort of cute-lover-kidding thing with Roger. So we were having a good time, but I was getting really tense because basically I couldn't get my mind around wearing a shirt on a hot summer night. I really wanted to "dress suitably" but still wear short shorts and show off my arms. Roger was getting a little annoyed, finally; it was sort of becoming an issue. Maybe I'm not being totally honest about this whole thing, though.

I should tell you that up to and before this dinner, there were other things on my mind. Like the fact that I had been seeing Cassidy out at the bar. Roger knew about Cassidy. I told him the whole story (except the part about him liking to be hit, and certainly not the scat part). He knew about how the police had been on my case and that Cassidy had been a loser and well… You know the way people talk about ex-boyfriends (even though Cassidy wasn't really a boyfriend) that makes them sound a little more awful then they really were? It's just like drugs. You know. People say — "Coke was so awful I could never do it any more." When the really honest thing to say is — "I loved coke, it was like heaven doing it. But I know I have to stop." Now if I was being rational and truly honest in talking to Roger about Cassidy, I would have said that I had unbelievable sex with him and that scared me. But you don't tell some beautiful new lover that you had unbelievable sex with somebody else. Maybe *good* sex or *fun* sex, but you don't want to build it up too much (oh my God, the more I talk about this the more I realize that being in a relationship involves so many lies, even when you're trying to be honest). So anyway, Roger knew about Cassidy. But he basically knew about him as a loser piece of dirt I had nothing to do with any more. And all that was basically true. But of course Roger didn't know what usually happened when I saw Cassidy in a bar.

The reason he didn't know is because I once made meeting up with Cassidy into a fun little performance for Roger. We were standing around *Woody's*, which is like this very middle-class place where beautiful hunks and Denton go, the last place you'd expect to see possible future Jerry Springer-guest types like Cassidy. But sure enough, Cassidy was there, making moon-eyes at me. So that was when I told Roger a lot about Cassidy and said, "Really act like my boyfriend now. I mean, you are. But let's really do it up so that Cassidy stays away from us." So we held hands all of a sudden and necked a bit and actually had fun: Roger had a great sense of humour. I told him to be sickening, and talk baby talk to me. And he did and it was neat. Like a little play. And I love good plays.

So that was great. I made seeing Cassidy into a whole thing that made us bond more. I even told my nice middle-class analyst about it and he seemed very pleased. Despite the fact that he just nodded and smiled (his basic thing).

But that wasn't all.

I had also seen Cassidy another time, and he had managed to talk dirty to me. It was just before the dinner. He came up to me in a sleazier bar (which I probably shouldn't have been in anyway, with my new life and everything) when I was totally unprepared and didn't have Roger to defend myself with. He didn't even say hello. He just whispered in my ear that he'd like to have my cock in his mouth, and he just kept talking about it. And I let him talk. It was all about how nice it felt and how we were made for each other, and how he might even like to take a shit for me.

And then he told me that he had his brother's van.

Yeah, I know that sounds innocent enough. But think about it for a minute: *his brother's van*. Well, the way Cassidy made it sound, this van was quite the sex palace. Apparently it was loaded with beer in this little fridge and everything and very comfortable and all curtained in at the back so no one could see. But the big thing about it was that the van was completely covered, on the inside, according to Cassidy, with white vinyl. Cassidy knew the effect that telling me this was going to have.

So Cassidy whispered to me that the van was covered in white vinyl. He went on about how it was very easy to clean up and, boy, how much he'd like to suck me off and take a shit on the white vinyl inside that van.

I can't tell you how hard this whole little conversation made me. It's like Cassidy, the stalker, had been storing up this fabulous fantasy for me. And now that he knew I was in love with Roger (we had already done the kissing thing in front of him) he was bringing out the heavy artillery. It worked all right. I'll admit I kissed him but good in the bar that night. I even started feeling his beautiful little ass, but then I just sort of pushed him — hard, I guess, because he sort of fell (but he *was* pretty drunk), and then I ran out of that bar.

So this had all happened just the night before the dinner. And it was very much on my mind.

But at the time, of course, I just figured this was God's way of testing me or something. Cassidy comes up with a white vinyl van at the very same time I have to go to this horrible dinner at Denton's house. It's like, well, if like, Jesus had to go through the seven temptations of whatever and at the same time be nailed to a wall. That's what was happening to me. But I could get through it. I could. I knew I could.

So that's what was going through my mind when we were having what was turning into our first fight — what I was going to wear to the damn dinner. So finally I end up wearing this vest. My favourite twenty-dollar Gap vest. I'm not ashamed to say that now and then I actually find clothing at The Gap. So this was my favourite dress-up vest because it showed my big muscled arms, but it still had a dressy quality because it was black and had little llamas and other sort of environmental, peaceful-type shit on it. The reason the vest was sort of a symbol of the whole dilemma of dressing was because some woman had once yelled at me when I was wearing it. Well she didn't actually yell, but it seemed like it.

I was at some dumb theatre company benefit launch party that I probably just went to so I could advance my career or meet a cute boy. As usual I didn't do either, so I was sort of peering into my wine, and I really hate wine: it gives me the shits (the bad kind, diarrhea). So I was feeling lousy and out of place and alone at this event and this crazy witchy woman comes up to me. She's obviously out of her mind because she's got a pad with her and she's writing in a public place. Any writer will tell you: no real writer writes in a public place. I doubt Hemingway ever wrote in a fucking Paris café, but I'm sure there are literary historians who will say I'm wrong. Okay, maybe *some* real writers write in public places, but I find that most of them don't. It's true that most of my friends are just playwrights or performance artists, but I've done a poll. I've asked them, "How many of you write in cafés or restaurants?" And they go, like, "Are you crazy?" I mean, how could you concentrate? Writing is a very intense, private thing, and if you do it in public you are either a very rare bird or else you're just showing off. Which is what I figured this woman was doing.

And I'm not saying she was a witch in a bad way. I mean witch in the literal sense. I mean, a lot of women are witches — that is, they practise white magic. Which is fine. I've got nothing against it. I mean, how the hell do you expect them to defend themselves in a fucking lousy stacked-deck misogynist man's world? But some witches are crazy (just like a lot of people in general are crazy) and this one seemed to be mad. So she sidled up to me (oh God, why do I always attract the nutty ones), and she goes, "Nice vest." And I thought, "She's a little nutty, but I can handle this, it's a compliment, I should try and be pleasant." But I have a whole history of people going crazy on me in public. They give me compliments and suddenly turn them into insults, so I'm careful.

There was this one guy who walked up to me and said, "I saw a play you were in and I thought it had the most beautiful moment in it I have ever seen." And me, buying the biscuit, I said, "Oh great, what moment?" And he said, "The moment when the boy's shirt was lying on the floor. That was the most beautiful moment I've ever seen." And I said, "Oh great, thanks, glad you liked it." I was beaming. And then he said, "The rest of the play was shit, but that moment with the shirt was fantastic." Then he just walked away. I felt as if I had just been kicked in the gut. I didn't get over it for weeks.

So when this witchy girl walked up and said, "Nice vest," I was of course paranoid and suspicious. And then she goes, "I wouldn't expect *you* to be wearing it, though." And I go, "Oh, why?" I wasn't being masochistic, just going for the sheer entertainment value of her wacky response. And she goes, "Well, because the vest has llamas on it, and they are a symbol of peace and you seem like such a menacing person." And then she, of course, disappeared. I waited for what seemed a respectable amount of time and then I just walked out of that goddamn benefit. Once I had been picked out as a "menacing" person it didn't seem like fun any more.

But you have to respect witches, because no matter how crazy they are they have a lot of power, and ever since then I've always thought that if I do look menacing to people (I can't help it — I'm big, I shave my head, I look good with a shaved head, so sorry if I look scary to you!) then if I wear my very peaceful llama vest that has been blessed by the witch, well, maybe I can counteract the strange menacing vibes which seem to freak some people out. So as you can see, the vest was sort of a symbol for me. It wasn't some ripped shirt. It was a semi-respectable article of clothing, one I could wear to this dinner to be myself and feel calm.

Well Roger wouldn't have it. He just didn't feel that a vest was right for the dinner party. I guess he was only thinking of me. He probably thought that Denton was going to treat me badly all night if I wore a vest to dinner, and he was trying to make it nice for me. That's what I like to think. Anyway, it became this big issue between us and we started to really fight. And I said, "Well I feel comfortable in this vest." But he was like, "For once could you just try and wear something that would make other people feel comfortable?" — stuff like that. So I finally gave in, after having a very faggoty hissy fit, and wore this goddamn leopard shirt that has sleeves that mostly cover my big arms. I mean, I look good in it. But it made me feel like I was twelve years old, like I was on my way to church or something.

It was right after this that I went to get the wine out of the fridge. And Roger saw that it was *Piat D'Or*. I thought he was going to have a conniption. "You bought *Piat D'Or*?" "Yes." "But I told you to get a nice wine." "This is a nice wine." "It's a #1!" (Sweetness.) "I know." "You have to bring a zero to a dinner party!" Well fuck me. I didn't know that. It seemed to make Roger so fucking upset; so we had to run off to the store and get more wine at the last minute and there was nothing open except local wine stores so we had to ride all the way up to an all-night liquor store and I let Roger pick out some god-damned Australian wine and he was happy.

And of course we're cabbing everywhere and spending money like there's no tomorrow, but I figure it's all because of this dinner and I'm doing it for Roger. I keep thinking: "This is my new life."

We got there late, of course, which I didn't think was such a big problem because I'd always believed it was chic to be late for dinner engagements. And of course Denton lives in an apartment with a doorman, so we had to check in. The doorman looked at us like we were criminals. I mean, Roger is not completely white, so I guess to racists he looks strange, even if he dresses like a college boy. And my arms were mostly covered up. But this young doorman, who's probably got no life at all, I mean, he's a doorman, looks at us like we're scum and we're going to rob the place. He seems very surprised when "Mr. Springfield" buzzes us up. We ride up in this elevator which is all mirrors. I hate that. But actually, it did make me think of having sex with Roger right there in front of the mirrors once I got over looking at myself in that leopard shirt. It's sexy, but conservative. (I was also wearing my long blue shorts. I bought them at The Gap too, and only wear them to my mother's house or summer funerals.) Finally we get to the next-to-the-top floor. I guess it was as close to the top as Denton could get without getting a fucking penthouse. I hate top-floor apartments because I'm always afraid I'm going to jump or push someone off; it sort of added to the tension.

We knock on the door, which has some sort of wreath on it, with summer flowers, and everything's already starting to drive me crazy. Denton opens the door and of course he's wearing white from head to toe.

"You're a little bit late."

"Sorry," says Roger. I tried to smile.

"Well, it's lucky I've cooked a dinner that can simmer."

Damn right we're lucky. I ask him what he's cooked and he says *coq au vin* and this really bugs me. Why can't he just say chicken in wine? Why does he use this faint little French accent when he announces it, and bounce on his toes like he wants to add to my nausea? God he's annoying. At least he approves of the wine. Oh how wonderful; I can't control my joy at his approval (who knows what shit might have hit the fan if we'd brought the *Piat D'Or*) and then he immediately grabs Roger and says, "I've got the new Charlie Pachter I was telling you about. You just have to see it. Excuse us, will you Jack?" And they run off into the bedroom (the same bedroom that Roger once stayed over in) and close the fucking door. Can you believe it? I mean, what am I, a fucking moron? Don't I know anything about modern art? I mean, I'm insecure, but when you hardly know someone, and they've just come to your apartment for dinner, don't you think it's, like, bad manners to run off with the guy's boyfriend and leave him standing alone in your living room?

I say this partially to justify my bad behaviour. I suppose what I did next was bad. I don't know. I was just being myself. And I figure, when you're feeling like a piece of shit, for whatever reason, it's best to be yourself in the most extreme way possible. So Denton has a TV, go figure, but it's sort of tucked away in a corner. In what they call "entertainment centres" these days. It's behind these closed doors and it has some Inuit artwork hung in front of it. But I find it. And then I figure where there's smoke there's… *dirty videos*. Denton must have dirty videos. I mean, he's not qualified to be a middle-class fag if he hasn't decided to spill some of that ever ready sperm on his own carpet instead of a backroom floor. Now I was feeling feisty, but *really*, I didn't mean to cause trouble. You have to understand that my values are so different from Denton's that, like, it seems impossible to me that certain things would upset him. But of course I did upset him.

So yes, I find, behind some books, I mean literally hidden, a pile of Jeff Stryker videos. Now I don't know if you know anything about gay porn, but you can tell a lot about a person by the video they keep. If they like Joey Stephano then they're a top who's into fucking young butt. If they like Danny Russo they're into very kinky sex. If it's Jeff Stryker, then we're dealing with somebody who is a major size queen (hence his friendship with Roger — these things are always important in a friendship), and we're also dealing with somebody who likes straight guys to abuse them. Because Jeff Stryker (if you've ever seen him) is basically this straight-acting dirty-talking top with an enormous dick who always tells guys to suck it. (I saw him in real life and the funny thing is he's incredibly short. Which makes his big dick a surprise. But the shortness thing, it's so funny. Because short guys make such funny topmen, the whole Napoleonic thing. Anyway, no, more power to the short guys who like to order people around. I've met some cute ones in my life who've ordered *me* around. Hey, it's just, well, now and then you look at a guy like that and think, "Hey, talk all you want guy, but you're short!" It sort of makes you laugh. I'm sure that's disrespectful to short people, but you've got to kid the macho short guys, they are really too much.)

Now Denton was obviously a Jeff Stryker aficionado.

He did not have just one or two flicks, he had about twenty. He even had the bisexual videos, which is a sure sign of obsession. You see, Jeff Stryker not only makes gay videos but a bunch of so called straight ones with pictures of girls with fake boobs on the cover. They're called things like *Bi-Coastal* or *The Big Switch* or some such crap. So the fact that Denton has done extensive research into Jeff Stryker is, to me, significant. Once I've done a good inspection, just on time, what should I hear but my boyfriend and Denton bouncing down the hall.

So Denton apologizes: "I'm sorry for stealing Roger like that..." (*stealing*, oh please) "but we'd been talking so much about this piece. Here, let me show you too…" And he gestures to the bedroom.

Now I have no desire to enter that horrible room where the two of them did or didn't do anything. So I say, "Hey, I'll pass. Is it another picture of the Queen?" Because Charlie Pachter's big joke is to paint and draw, like, hundreds of pictures of Queen Elizabeth. Anyway, my joke makes nobody laugh. In fact, Roger kind of frowns. And Denton looks very miffed and says: "No, in fact, he's doing a lot of new work, boys in Florida." Well, in fact, I wouldn't mind seeing Charlie's new pictures of boys in Florida, but the mention of boys just makes me remember how hot I am to ask Denton about his porn collection. So I do. Denton is obviously not pleased. "How did you find that?" he asks.

"Well, a fag without a porn collection is kind of like a canoe without a paddle. I see you are a complete size queen." Denton looks at Roger.

"And where do you get that idea?"

"Well, Roger baby, this guy has, like, the whole *oeuvre* of Jeff Stryker. Even the bisexual flicks. Now tell me, Denton: do you find it, like, politically incorrect when he says, 'Suck my dick, you little faggot?' Or does it just make you come?"

I swear, Roger and Denton look at me like I'd just taken a shit on the floor. Which, of course (I had controlled myself), I had not done.

"I'm not really into analyzing pornography," says Denton.

Well, I'd like to feel bad at how lousily we're getting along, but this kind of talk, and his prissy, nasty little tone, just makes me mad. So I say, "Roger is. He's a big fan of Czech pornography. Aren't you, Roger? All those hung Eastern Europeans. And it sounds like they're abusing you backwards when they talk."

Now I thought that was really a funny remark — you know, something approaching fancy faggot dinner table-type wit. Which I obviously didn't know anything about. I was referring to how Russian always sounds like backwards talk. But this got even fewer laughs than the Pachter quip. Everything I said was just getting me into more trouble.

Denton goes, "I think we should eat." And Roger looks relieved. So now we all tramp over to the table which looks so fucking beautiful. Yes it does, I have to admit. Denton has seated Roger beside him. It's so horrible, and I feel like they're both watching me. They are. Now I don't know if I mentioned this, but I have terrible table manners. And it's not the way my mother brought me up (don't blame her), it's just that I'm kind of a pig. What can I say? When it's time to eat, it's time to eat. I just dig in. And to me the point of eating is taste, right? And you want to get as much taste as fast as possible. So, like, I basically shovel in the food. And there was a nice salad there with big lumps of cheese in it, and it looked great so I just started shovelling. Roger and Denton look at each other really pointedly as they put their napkins in their laps. (I'm not kidding: simultaneously.) And I go, "What's wrong?" And Denton says, "You *should* save the dessert fork for your dessert."

I cannot believe he said that. I cannot fucking believe he said that. And all I can think of is this story my mother told me once. It was about how she went for dinner at my great aunt's house (that's my father's dad's sister), her name was Aunt Harriet. And Aunt Harriet put my mother (who was seventeen years old and just married at the time) at the front of the table and made her lead the whole dinner because the person sitting at the head was like the head person and had to lead everything. And she put the finger bowl down beside my mother and my mother didn't know what to do with it because she was a poor farm girl. So I just couldn't believe this, because I was feeling like a poor farm girl too. I looked at Roger, and he actually did seem to be a bit shocked at Denton. I mean, I know I'm a pig, but to criticize me for using the wrong silverware? That was a bit much. At this point I knew that Denton just completely hated me and that the whole evening was going to be horrible because this man was a sad old jealous fag, who probably wanted Roger all to himself. I was the dreadful interloper, the sexual farm girl with bad manners who was stealing away his pretty little boy. Some fags are so fucked. I swear. Well, Denton reacts to what is obviously shock from Roger and tones down his remark. "But I suppose it doesn't really matter. You boys just finish your salad and I'll work on the main course." Actually, looking back on it, I can't believe that Denton served the salad first. That's supposed to be *so* uncontinental.

So Roger, at least, still doesn't seem to have lost his sense of humour. I mean, he's giving me sort of fake puppy-dog eyes and whispering, "Be nice." I say, "Hey I'm trying, but he's such an asshole." And Roger says, "He's intimidated by you." Right, because I'm a famous fag actor and everything. But I won't buy this one. "He's in love with you," I say. "No he's not," says Roger.

But I look in his eyes and I think he knows it's true.

And this is the part where I get really sad. Because I know it might not sound like it but I was really trying. You have to imagine me wearing clothes I hate wearing, at some fag's house that I would never visit, being corrected on my table manners, and not hitting the roof. I was doing all this for Roger because I thought maybe it was possible for us to be lovers. I was doing my best. And this little nubby peppy asshole was ruining our whole relationship.

So what does he do next? He does something that really makes me mad. He brings the dinner in on General Idea plates. Do you know what they are? Well, General Idea is this really cool bunch of artists who do this kind of camp art. I really like their stuff because it's sarcastic, but still really felt. And two of these artists have died of AIDS already, and they do really good stuff about AIDS and being queer, and what can I say, I think their art is right-on. Anyway, I feel very strongly about General Idea, and they made these beautiful plates that are just done in lovely colours. But they're made to go on a wall, right? I mean, it's art. You're not supposed to eat off the fucking things.

I think it was something about the *coq au vin*, which looks like poop anyway, just plopped into the middle of these beautiful plates because Denton wanted to make a goddamned impression. I mean, these plates are incredibly expensive. Like three hundred dollars apiece or something. So if you're serving dinner on them you are just making a major money statement. Like, "I am so cultured and smart but mainly so rich that I can afford like ten of these goddamn plates and serve dinner on them." So when Denton came in carrying those plates, well, I wanted to cry, because I knew that what I was about to do was going to cause major trouble and probably break up me and Roger. But I just couldn't help myself. I just lost control. Besides, I was very confused. On the one hand I was trying to start a new life, but I just couldn't understand why God would give me this kind of test. How could I put up with someone like Denton without making a squawk? So I just blew up. I just blew up right at Denton. But first I asked him, "Are those General Idea plates?"

And Denton goes, "Yes, don't you just love them?"

And then I start yelling and I stand up, and poor Roger looks like he's going to cry, and I say: "Yeah, of course I love them! But they happen to be works of art, you fucking moron."

And Denton says, "Are you calling me a moron?" And I say, "Yeah Denton, I am. I'm sorry Roger, I have to say this. But anybody who serves dinner on a fucking General Idea plate is a complete fucking idiot because they are works of art that belong on the goddamn wall! You're not supposed to put your shitbrown food on them, and the only reason you're doing it is to show off how much fucking money you have and that makes me want to puke and…"

And then Roger got up and interrupted me, but it didn't work. I just looked at him and he knew that I was saying goodbye to him in my own sad angry way because I didn't know what else to do. This whole

Denton thing was just too big a rift between us, and I kept yelling about Toller Cranston: I don't know why. "And I notice you've got some nice Toller Cranston pictures on your fucking walls, Denton. Could you be any more of a fucking cliché? Do you just collect stuff by famous people or do you actually have any taste? No, I don't think you have any taste at all. You're just a guy who likes to get abused. That's obvious from your fucking taste in videos, and you are in love with my boyfriend, and if my boyfriend is such good friends with such a mean stupid pretentious son of an asshole, then he's not my boyfriend any more! Fuck you." And then I slammed my salad across the table. Roger yelled after me, but I was already at the door. And at the door I really lost it.

"He's got Eskimo scuplture Roger! Eskimo fucking sculpture. I mean this is not the real thing, this is stuff that you buy at the Colonnade! If the Colonnade still exists! This is like oppression of your people! This guy oppresses your people!" And Roger looked at me like I had lost my mind, which I had, because it was basically a lame argument. (But that's what you do at moments like this when you know your life is falling apart and you're mad, at yourself really; you make lame arguments.) I mean the Eskimo art that Denton had really wasn't that bad, but I was just using anything I could to get Roger to side with me. But my desperation was more than obvious. And then I ran out.

The first thing I thought I should do was go and see Barb. I thought, "Fuck, she's my closest friend; really, she's like my only friend." And I thought Barb would be able to talk me out of this, I mean, I thought mainly Barb would be able to talk me back to Roger because, of course, what I was really feeling, the real feeling I had, was, *is there anywhere I could find a van, where I could find myself that nice clean white van?*

No, I swear, that was really on my mind. It was like after defiling Denton's fucking dinner party all I wanted to do was find Cassidy and that van. And that really scared me. It really fucking scared me. So I thought, "Barb, she's my saviour." She helps me through things, she may be straight and everything, but she knows men are pigs. She understands temptation. She has some respect for how hard it is to stop dating a creep, so she could help me. If anyone could get me to apologize to Roger, she could. I just know she could. So I ran out of the goddamn apartment building and the doorman looked at me like, "Oh, I was right; he is some sort of a thug." I think I yelled at him — "Fuck you!" Anyway, that's how out of my mind I was when I got in a taxi and bombed over to Barb's.

Now Barb lives by the beach and Denton was like, of course, in the middle of yuppie hell, so it was almost a twenty-minute, incredibly expensive ride. Hell, I didn't even know if she was going to be there.

The cab driver was this incredibly nice laid-back guy who just made me furious. Have you ever noticed how at peace with the world some cab drivers are? The only time I ever take cabs is when I've just lost my mind for some reason or other, and I have to get somewhere fast. And there's always this guy driving who's, like, a part-time experimental filmmaker, and married, with a gorgeous kid, and they're very relaxed and I always feel like an intense hysterical fag in the back seat. And of course, as usual, the cab driver has seen me in *Pookie the Prawn*. Yes, I have to admit, I was on this TV show called *Pookie the Prawn* a few times. I needed to supplement my income. Well, actually, supplement isn't the word. In order to give myself an income I do

TV shows when I can get them. And believe it or not, I'm on *Pookie the Prawn*. It's this show for kids about a giant prawn who's kind of goofy. And they had big local actors to do guest spots and they asked me to play the Genie. Now normally I would have been complimented, but I felt it was also like, "Let's get a fag for this role," because the Genie is basically gay. Oh yeah, whenever you see a genie in anything, you know that. I mean, he gets whoever he's talking with to rub the lamp and we know what *that's* all about. So anyway, I was on this program for kids and it was a bit of a scandal, and people actually wrote letters to the newspaper and stuff and complained that I was a bad influence on kids. Well *of course* I was a bad influence on kids. I was the fucking *Genie*. I was the bad guy and kids were supposed to learn from Pookie's adventures with me what *not* to do. People are so stupid sometimes. So this cab driver, of course, had seen me on *Pookie the Prawn*, and he said, "Hey, aren't you the Genie?" And it just made me so furious. Basically because this guy was so centred and loving and generous, and for sure straight on top of it all, that he could have a relaxed conversation with me when I was hysterical. But I said, "Yeah, I was the Genie." And I gave him a big tip even though I was extremely jealous of him for being so obviously centred and having such a nice life.

And then I was at Barb's, praying that she would be home. Sure enough, she was. Thank God she was. She opened the door and then I was in a real place. A real, messy house. A place someone lived in. And the art on the walls was stuff she really liked, not just stuff she'd read about in a book.

Barb was, like, having an evening at home, which is one of the things I love about her. I mean, I am almost constitutionally incapable of having an evening at home, but Barb was like all curled up with her dog Boner. Her dog was called Boner, and she was completely cool with that, which is great. I mean, she called her dog Boner and it was a real litmus test. Because on the one hand, it's a totally suitable name for a dog. But on the other, it's a dirty name too. So you can tell the sexual people from the non sexual ones just by how they react to the dog's name. Like the old ladies go: "Oh Boner, how cute. Come here, sweet little Boner." Whereas people like me go, "Wow, you named your dog after a hard-on! How completely cool."

And Boner was kind of an ugly boxer-type dog, the kind that always made me feel comfortable. He usually peed on me because he was so excited. This always made Barb happy. Once he even took a shit when he saw me. Barb said this meant he really liked me; she had no idea how appropriate it was.

This was what I needed, Barb's incredible centredness. She's not a saint or anything. It's just that, well, she always had that uncanny straight woman's knack for now and then just saying: "Fuck, who needs sex?" Do you know what I mean? (I think it's because their straight boyfriends are always undersexed. As far as I can tell, from talking to straight women, it's all a big myth about women having headaches. It's the men who have the headaches all the time.) I don't mean that she was unsexual — far from it. If she *had* been I couldn't have possibly been friends with her. She was actually kind of a sex fiend, and frank about it. Even though men always think she's uptight because she's

Asian and has a British accent. I mean I've known Barb to take home men who wanted a relationship, and then she would be like, "That's fine, we fucked, now get out." The next day, no breakfast or anything. I mean most gay men would do breakfast at least, just so they wouldn't *look* like an insensitive cliché. But Barb was perfectly happy just making it with a guy. Then she'd be totally freaked when they wanted something more and deeper. Which means that guys were always wanting something more and deeper with her. But even though she had this wacky, vulnerable quality, she was also completely cool and would sometimes be this really happy single woman with Boner and her TV and her books and her hot baths and her tea. No sexual desire at all. I mean, I have to say that at times I wondered about her and Boner. Like, she was so incredibly comfortable with Boner's bodily functions. And also because Boner was named that because of his, you know, boner. I sometimes wondered if it was possible that they could have had some sort of, and don't take this the wrong way, sexual relationship. Well actually, do take it the wrong way. I mean, Barb was always frank about how she loved getting her cunt licked (by guys), and sometimes when I left her apartment at night she'd be laying there incredibly comfortably with her dog, and I'd think, "Hey, I wonder if they're going to have some sort of fun."

I know that sounds horrible and impossible but it's not that far fetched. I used to know this guy that jerked off his dog. He's a famous rock star now. I just say that to impress you because I know you don't believe that anyone, much less a rock star, would jerk off his dog. But this guy was really good friends with his dog and he said his dog got horny all the time and he felt sorry for him and the only way to relieve his dog's erection was to jerk him off. I mean, this guy had a very special relationship with his pet (it was obviously a gay dog). And Barb also had a very special relationship with Boner, who was obviously heterosexual.

Anyway, the relevant thing here was that I was hysterical and looking for help, and Barb was in one of her completely relaxed and single moods and this is what I needed. I just loved Barb's flat. It was furnished with all these great little knick-knacks. Because, well, basically Barb was a thief. It was one of the things I really respected about her. She could get away with it really easily because she could look very Asian if she wanted to, and with her sweet British accent she could appear very uptight and proper. So she was like the last person anybody ever thought would steal anything. Often she'd go to a store in a kind of ethnic muu-muu, looking very Guyanese, and pick up anything she could steal.

It was another way that Barb and I really connected. I mean, she didn't know about my obsession with, shall we say, the darker aspects of sex and stuff, and she had been shocked when I showed her my asshole when she was drawing me; but she did have this sleazy side that stole stuff, and I really respected that. Besides, she only stole from chains and rich stores. You know, stores where it just seemed criminal to be selling things for, like, a hundred dollars. I mean she had a hundred-dollar box of stones that smelled like Eucalyptus. You're just supposed to put them in your bathroom and they'll smell beautiful forever. They feel great and there's little wooden acorns thrown in to boot. Now a thing like this is something you would never buy for a hundred dollars. But you certainly might steal it. It was great for me too, because Barb was always giving me nice stolen things. My apartment looked much better for it.

So she was all wrapped in her blanket and she had this beautiful mug that she had stolen, and she was drinking herbal tea. She looked so beautiful, and I knew she was going to be my saviour. Sometimes straight people can be so sensible: I knew that my Barb would be. That's what I came for. *Sense and Sensibility* (Jane Austen was her favourite author).

"So what's up?" asks Barb, as she leads me into her big living room — lots of plants and warm rugs and stolen knick-knacks. I tell her the whole story. That I was so in love with Roger (which she knew), but that I had been seeing Cassidy now and then at the bars and he was driving me crazy. That I was very tempted by him. And I told her that I was trying to make it work with Roger but he insisted that I befriend the most horrible monster of a fag that God had ever created. She kind of skrinkled up her nose.

"What's so horrible about Denton again?" "Oh he's just..." I tried to explain what a nightmare he was, and how uptight and judgemental and nasty he was, and how he just wanted Roger to himself. And then she started saying stuff that definitely ended up freaking me out.

"He sounds like a creep," she said, twisting the corner of this gorgeous Oriental-style throw that she had on the couch: she had actually worn it out of this fancy store one day, and no one noticed — they thought it was her dress. "I mean, he does sound like a creep, but really, it sounds to me like you went to that dinner almost wanting to have a fit."

I didn't like the turn this talk was taking at all. I really hated it. But of course I couldn't stop listening.

"Do you want some tea?" she asked. No, I didn't.

"What do you mean, brought it on myself?" And she went on: "You know, I think you've got these demons in you and when people have demons they have to confront them. Did I tell you about me and sleazy black men?" I said no, I didn't know what she was talking about. And then she tells me the most bizarre thing: "Well, I've always been drawn to black men and I've hated it in myself because I thought it was racist. And then I decided desire can't be racist. I just have a thing for them. So I walked into this bar, it was an unbelievably sleazy place, very low-life, completely filled with nothing but gorgeous black men. And all I had to do was sail in there and take my pick. I knew they were all pimps and drug addicts. It was that kind of place. I, of course, was incredibly exotic to them. And I took home this enormous, sexy black man and well, I might as well tell you, he did crack at my place. But the thing is, I wanted him so badly, I didn't care."

Oh my God, I thought I'd come to my one steady friend, my one straight friend, because she'd give me sensible advice and here she is now, hanging around in sleazy bars, picking up crack addicts. Could my timing have been worse? So I told her that I was, like, amazed at this change in her life. I mean charmingly wacky Barb picking up a crack addict. Uptight on the outside, wild on the inside. Barb, who got so freaked out drawing my asshole, was picking up crack addicts. "Did you do any?" I asked.

"I did, actually," said Barb. "What was it like?" "It was amazing," she said. "I could get addicted just like that." "So, doesn't that scare you?" I asked. "You're thinking you went too far, right? You crossed some limit or something, and you should just turn back?" I was fucking desperate for her to be sensible. "No," she said. "No, I'm tired of everybody thinking I'm uptight. I'm tired of going home with middle-class white guys who are freaked when I don't sleep with them again. I'm tired of French guys who are really Portuguese. I mean, this is dangerous, but this is fundamental, this is real."

I do not want to hear this. I can't believe, in fact, that Barb is talking to me this way. How can she? She was supposed to be this nice, mothering person. That's what she usually is. What was going on? I decided to be frank. "Barb, I'm getting very freaked out by this conversation. I came here because I thought you would give me some sensible advice, and tell me I should apologize to Denton and go back with Roger. If you don't do that, then I might do something crazy. I might go find Cassidy."

"So what's so terrible about Cassidy?"

"The sex with him is very dark, we get into very dark things."

"Like what? I'm not shy." This is the woman who refused to draw my gaping asshole. I could not tell her.

"Whatever it is, it can't be all that bad. You're obviously completely drawn to him. Jack, you're like me, you've been uptight all your life. That's what this whole gay-lib, gay actor drag thing is about for you. Loosening up. Hasn't your therapist told you that? Just loosen up. If a dark side is there, you might as well deal with it. It won't go away."

"But what about if it consumes you?"

"It won't consume you. That just happens in bad movies."

"Really? I think people get consumed all the time." I looked at her, my last chance for the sensible lecture, which I obviously wasn't going to get. "If you don't stop me, I'm going to go out and find Cassidy."

"Well," she said, and there was love in her eyes. I

really think there was love in her eyes. "You do whatever you really want to do. I think that's what's important."

Oh Barb. Fucking Barb. You have no idea. Why did I have to get you on the night after you'd just smoked crack with some hugely endowed sex fiend. I was furious with her for giving me the wrong advice, but then I just realized that I couldn't really be mad because it wasn't her fault; it was all mine. Mine for wanting, well, I might as well admit it, because you know it, I wanted to run off and find Cassidy and get him to suck my cock and take a shit in the white van.

"Excuse me," I said, "I've got to go." And she was like, "Oh no! You just got here and Boner will be so disappointed." But I didn't care about Boner. I didn't care about her goddamn dog's feelings now. Nothing mattered but finding Cassidy.

I said goodbye very quickly, and when I left the doorstep of her lovely little flat with the stolen stained glass figurines hanging in the window, I knew that I had left something forever.

I was consumed completely by horniness, and I don't know if you've ever been in that state. It isn't so much that I had a hard-on, it's that I was just totally obsessed with Cassidy and everything I wanted to do with him. Maybe I might even tie him up a bit. Maybe I would fuck him for the first time. Maybe I might even bash him around.

The night was crisp, it had really cooled down, and there was danger in the air. You know, like when the leaves are just sort of rustling a bit and anything might happen. It was one of those late summer nights when fall was approaching, you could feel it.

I hopped into a cab and I got a complete Jamaican stoner driver, which seemed so appropriate after Barb. I wondered if she was going to fuck him next, and I was happy, because I began to feel as stoned as this fucking cab driver, thinking, yeah, everybody should fuck everybody, that's what should happen, that's the way things should be.

When I got to my house, the first thing I saw, of course, was the van. I looked at it, and it could have been anybody's van. But it was white and it had a serpent painted on the side. Of course it was Cassidy's brother's van. That was exactly the kind of corny thing that Cassidy's brother would have painted on it, for sure. The van was parked next to my building in a little side alley, next to a very tall apartment complex with no windows. There was a light shining from somewhere that kind of highlighted it. As I got closer, I could hear the van purring. Oh, that was a sexy sound. And I could see Cassidy at the wheel.

I could also hear the radio playing. It was some sort of fuck music, the kind of corny music that Cassidy liked. It was all too perfect. I was in a hurry, though I didn't know why. When Cassidy saw me he started to smile. I knew he wanted everything I had to give him. I told him to get out of the van. For some reason he decided to keep the van running, and I liked the sound of it. It comforted me. I dragged him to the end of the alley, which was just behind the van. Then I started to kiss him. Each time I kissed him, I slapped him. And each time I slapped him, Cassidy said, "Don't do that." But the thing is, I knew he really wanted me to do it. So I slapped him over and over, again and again, and I kissed him too. And I was punishing him for making me want him so much, for making me do these things, for wanting his sweet ass, for wanting his sweet shit, for wanting his sweet everything.

And for a moment it seemed, just for a moment, that I wasn't guilty, which was a very new sensation. I just felt so free when I slapped him, but it was getting to the point where he was bleeding and he wasn't talking very well. His speech was sort of slurred as he tried to say, "Don't do that." His voice was weaker, hardly comprehensible. But I kept kissing him on his bloody mouth and the blood was warm, and then I started pushing him against the wall, though I wasn't hitting his head against the wall. I didn't want to kill him, I swear I didn't want to kill him at that point, I just wanted to fuck the living daylights out of him, and I could tell he was ready for it.

Then I did something that I still don't completely understand. I went back up to the van and I got in on the driver's side. I don't know why I didn't take Cassidy with me. I remember shouting at him. Expecting him to come. And of course he didn't. And then I got in, and I started the van. No, I don't understand why I started the van. Where was I going to go without Cassidy?

But the van didn't go forward, it went backward.

And I heard a noise and then I knew it was Cassidy and I had to get out of the van and I got out and I ran and I ran and I ran.

I say I can't explain what I did because it's true that even though I remember getting in the van, I don't remember why, or what really happened. I mean, the whole thing, from getting in the van (into the driver's seat), to driving, and then getting out and running, I mean, all I really remember is hitting Cassidy and running. I don't remember anything after that, hardly anything at all.

It's not clear.

I mean, I might have gotten in the van. But why did I get in the van, without Cassidy, in the driver's side, if I wanted to fuck his ass?

It doesn't make any sense.

So I ran. Though I didn't know where to go. I couldn't head back to Roger's — he hated me. I couldn't go to Barb's. I mean, this was the woman who said, "Confront your dark side." She'd probably urge me to run back and eat Cassidy's bloody body. Christ, everything was so crazy. So I called up this old friend of mine, Tony. He's a publicist who works for *Phantom of the Opera* and he's really nice.

Yeah, that's what I did. I knocked on Tony's door. At whatever time it was, two in the morning or something. Tony's a really nice normal guy who works 9 to 5 publicizing theatre, and he has a wonderful lover and everything, and he let me sleep on his couch. I used to date Tony and he always liked and admired me. I knew I'd be comfortable there and that Tony wouldn't ask any questions.

I got up in the morning and Tony had left a lovely note and he had bacon and stuff put aside for me so I could make myself a wonderful breakfast, and I did. It was very strange. It all seemed like a dream. Actually, I pretty well had myself convinced that it was a dream. It seemed to me that I had gotten drunk or stoned sometime in the night (even though I couldn't remember where or when), and walked home and then seen Cassidy. It freaked me out, and then I just came to Tony's because I didn't want to be stalked by Cassidy any more.

At least that's what I knew I would tell the police.

Because I had a pretty strong feeling that the police

were going to come back into my life. And it was
pretty important that I try and remember what had
happened. It was tough, because the whole thing, as
the day wore on, did seem like a dream. I went home,
and Cassidy's white van wasn't there, and I went out
later in the afternoon and even examined the alley.
There was no sign of anything. There was no news. I
checked on TV, the local news that always starts out
with local death and destruction just to get your
attention. There was nothing about Cassidy being
dead. I mean, I probably didn't even kill him. I
thought, "Well, maybe for some reason I got in the
van. But no way I killed him." In fact, I probably left
Cassidy in the alley after slapping him around, and
then just ran off. So Cassidy probably just drove the
van away. Like before, when he was almost strangled.
He bounced back. It took a lot to kill Cassidy.

Yeah, that's it. And slapping Cassidy really was just
self-defence anyway. Because he had been stalking me.

So it was almost unreal now, because I kept telling
myself over and over again that I dreamed it: driving
Cassidy against the wall, killing him with the white
van. Yeah, this was the beginning of a period of my
life when I wasn't quite sure what was real and what
was a dream.

There was this kernel planted in my brain: all my
life I had known I was guilty of something, right? I
had known. I had known I was like Montgomery Clift
in *A Place In The Sun*. And now there was, I guess,
what philosophers would call an objective corollary
(see, I do read!). There was an actual thing that
related to my guilt. I was guilty of doing something
specific. I didn't just hate God in my imagination,
and I didn't just feel guilty about maybe showing my
asshole to Barb.

Maybe I had actually *done* something. All I could think about was: Did I do it, or didn't I? And sometimes it seemed that I had, and I was subsumed with guilt, and that everybody knew, or that they would find out, and that the police would get me. And then at other moments I thought: "No, you're crazy. This is your nice apartment. You're going to have breakfast. You're going to see your friends tonight. You're going to be a normal person. You have nothing to worry about. Cassidy was stalking you; Cassidy's a freak. If anyone killed him in an alley, well, then it wasn't you. You might have beat him up. But that's natural anger because Cassidy was on your tail. The police know that, the police know that Cassidy was crazy. They know he was driving you crazy."

But certain really horrible thoughts also came into my head. Like the idea that nobody would really care if Cassidy lived or died. I know that sounds like a terrible thing to think, and it was, but basically you have to understand that I would only think this late at night, when I'd wake up suddenly, you know, the way you do sometimes, and say to myself, "Oh my God, I've killed someone, and everyone knows about it, and the police are going to get me." And then I'd worry about it some more, and I'd think: "No, it's been a week now. No one has said anything. And you haven't heard that Cassidy's dead." No, there were no signs up in the Ghetto looking for a "gay killer." I mean, look at Andrew Cunanan. People love this shit. They'd have pictures of me on CNN by now.

And then all I could think about was how I'd danced shirtless at so many gay parties. For sure that seemed to be what straight people saw as a real sign of guilt, or at least of ultimate sinfulness.

And it was at these moments, when I would just be

turning the whole thing over and over in my mind, that I'd wonder, "Was I awake or was I asleep when it happened?" Maybe I really had fallen asleep and dreamed the whole thing. It sure seemed like a dream. And maybe, well, even if I did kill Cassidy, who cared? No, really, that's how desperate I was to get away from the guilt, to kill it. I'd think, "Well, maybe his mother cared about him. But who's his mother? Some low-class drunk who probably didn't know one day from the next anyway." I *know* these are horrible thoughts, but I thought them, and I also thought, "Well, how did Cassidy enrich the world?" I actually compared myself to him and thought, "Here I am an actor and a drag queen and performer and all these things, and I've brought some joy into people's lives, and Cassidy didn't even have a job. I mean he just was a sort of drifter/grifter. He never *did* anything. He sort of begged, borrowed and stole things, and that's why everybody hated him. Besides, lots of people had tried to kill him. So what does it really matter anyway that he's dead?" I know those are disgusting thoughts. But then I thought of this play I'd seen once, about a psychopathic killer who told a psychiatrist that his victim was a worthless person. And I couldn't believe I was actually thinking the same thing as a justification.

But other times, having a corollary, a reason for my guilt, was incredibly freeing. I'd lie in bed at night and think, "At last I know *why* I'm guilty! I don't have to go through this over and over again any more." I mean, I feel guilty all the time for the stupidest things, like breaking a date with someone. I mean, I'm the type of person who actually feels guilty crossing the road. I'm not kidding. Every time I cross the road, and, you know, some big-assed car is waiting to turn the corner, I actually feel so bad because the car can't get across. I actually accuse myself of being some lazy, slow-walking pedestrian holding up cars that need to get places fast. And then I have to tell myself, "No, you have a right to be a pedestrian. To walk where you want. I mean, you don't even have as much money as these assholes who drive cars." And then I get cocky and think, "Make those straight, rich, probably racist assholes in their stupid big cars wait for you! You're a good person." Yeah, these are the types of things I've turned over and over in my mind every goddamn day. When I was a kid I was so guilty I never even masturbated. No, really. It proved to be a real disadvantage when I became a homosexual. I mean, Okay, I had had orgasms. But the first one just happened one night when I was rubbing against the bed, lying on my stomach. I came and I thought I had peed the bed — which made me feel very guilty, of course. And from then on — once I figured out it was an orgasm — I would always rub myself against the bed in order to get off.

But I never rubbed or touched my cock. I remember it very distinctly. Every night when Larry Solway (this talk show host) was on my radio, and my mother was downstairs making out with her boyfriend (she was divorced from my father, but that's not why I'm a homosexual and/or a murderer; please leave my poor mother out of this), I would be rubbing myself against the bed until I came. Larry Solway was one of those loudmouth precursors to Howard Stern, and it seemed his radio shows were always about homosexuality. I remember one where Larry Solway said: "I think all homosexuals are probably narcissists, they all love themselves and want to have sex with themselves." And I remember it seemed to make a lot of sense to me as I was rubbing myself against the bed. Even though that's kind of a contradiction, because I was doing such a hugely unnarcissistic thing, masturbating without touching myself. Anyway, when I first touched an erect cock I kind of didn't know what to do with it because I had never touched my own. I know it sounds stupid, me getting guilty about little things like this — crossing the street and masturbating. But with me it's exponential. It starts there and gets worse.

It's not like this stupid *Oprah* episode I saw recently. It was all about confessing your guilt. They had all these middle-class people on, confessing the things they were most guilty about. And the things were, I'm not kidding, they were like, putting gum under the seat at the movies, and stealing towels from hotels and glasses from restaurants. And one woman was guilty because she always woke up to check her husband's breathing when he was sleeping at night. Great. How difficult it must be to confess to something like that. You're a saint who worries about whether your husband's still breathing. Right. And then Oprah herself made this big confession. That's always what the show is about: Oprah telling you some personal detail, so you feel like you're her fucking friend. So Oprah goes, "I feel guilty about the fact that sometimes when I'm all by myself I just close the curtains and dance around to my favourite song, *I'm Every Woman.*" Oh yeah, the things middle-class people get guilty about, like putting the garbage out on the wrong night, just make me so sick because I am really guilty, always guilty, guilty every minute about the silliest things — and the most horrible things. So at last I could think: "I don't have to worry whether I'm guilty or not, or think about why I'm so bad, because now I know in my heart of hearts that I am guilty. I did something horrible. I did the most horrible thing. I killed someone." It made me feel a new kind of relief. "Just give up," I thought. "Go to the cops, tell them, and you'll have more relief still."

But I didn't. I mean, part of it was I didn't want to be one of those compulsive confessors. No, I *know* I'm guilty. There is positive proof. But I just didn't want to be one of those people I've heard about who goes around confessing to everything only to have it turn out that they didn't do anything. I mean, they clog up the court system. And I would probably feel very guilty about that.

As you can see, I was very back and forth about the whole thing. But I thought, of course, that going back and forth and being tortured by all this, was a sure sign of guilt.

Roger tried to phone me but I didn't answer his calls. Once I saw Denton bouncing down the street and I wanted to kill him. But I didn't.

And I didn't want to talk to Barb. What was I going to say to her? She told me to do it, practically. And my therapist? Well I did try to tell him. During one of my worst moments I said: "Doctor, I have this dream where I've killed someone!" And he said, "Don't worry about it. That's good; it just means change."

It sure does.

So this went on for about a month and I was going pretty crazy. But there was a part of me thinking, "Well, this is the way it is. This is the way the rest of your life is going to be. You can handle it." And of course I thought of all the old movies. I thought of Montgomery Clift and I thought of Rosalind Russell and I even thought of Lana Turner in *The Postman Always Rings Twice*. That was a car thing too. She took her worthless but sweet husband out in a car, drunk, and then pushed him off a cliff. And that got me freaked out because in the movie her colour was white, her colour was always white, and her white purse, clean as anything, pure as snow, was found at the scene of the crime. And of course nobody thought it was odd that she would bring her purse to the scene of a crime to commit murder. But that freaked me out: white. You know, the white van I wanted Cassidy to take a shit in. White vinyl. Cassidy. Scat. But he never did. He never did.

And then, of course, it happened. My phone rang. (My phone is white — isn't that crazy?)

It was the police.

I didn't think it was the cops at first, because they were so cheery, and it was a man. I mean, I was used to the police being women now, and I was used to all those mother associations I developed with the cops who questioned me before, so to me it seemed odd and almost unreal that a police*man* would phone me. The comforting thing about the phone call was that even though I was surprised the cop was a man, it made me feel better somehow. Because, well, it couldn't be the same cops as before: the ones who had such control over my life because they were women who could make me confess.

This was a male voice, so I was safe. But one thing I didn't really notice when I got the initial phone call was that this male voice also sounded very much, oddly enough, like the woman officer from before. Very cheery, very nice. Almost like the same voice, only a bit deeper.

Anyway, the man wanted to meet me for lunch. And I thought, "Well, this is a man, this is the police. It's probably because Cassidy is dead and I knew Cassidy. So he's just calling me because he's checking up on Cassidy and all the people who knew him. And since I obviously knew Cassidy before, because they interviewed me when he got strangled, that's why they want to talk to me now. It's probably very innocent." I agreed to meet him for lunch.

And then of course it occurred to me that I'd better not reveal that I knew (or thought I knew, I mean, *maybe* I knew) that Cassidy was dead. Because it hadn't been in the papers or anything. So if I acknowledged it then I was guilty for sure. I realized I should have acted shocked that the police wanted to see me at all. Then I remembered it had only been a year since Cassidy had been strangled and left for dead, so I could pretend that I thought that it would be all about their ongoing investigation into a crime that had never been solved.

There. It wouldn't be so bad.

The day and night before the interview were torture. I didn't know what I was going to wear, how to act. I'd never felt so guilty. I thought everything I did would give me away. And then, of course, everything changed. I wasn't even a bundle of nerves. I wasn't even that upset. A smooth sort of calm came over me, and I really had decided to accept my fate. I think I was beginning to move into one of those "Oh I'm so relieved to find out what I'm guilty about" moods.

We decided to meet in this restaurant that was right by the theatre where I was performing at the time. It was a nice Jamaican place and everything was very relaxed there, and I thought it would make me feel normal. I got there a little late. I didn't think it would be right for me to be early: it might look like I was tortured by guilt. So I sort of casually strolled in, wanting it to look like I had a lot of time. That I could answer any questions he had. That I was that relaxed. Well, I walked in the door in my everyday just-going-for-a-lunch-only-this-time-with-a-police-man way, and suddenly there he was.

And this totally freaked me out.

The policewoman was a man.

What I'm talking about is this. The woman who interviewed me before, who was one of the female cops, was sitting in front of me now. Only this time she wasn't a she; she was a he. It was the same person, I swear. I remember thinking before that she was kind of a cheery woman in a suit. Now she was a cheery guy in a suit. It completely fucked me up.

Naturally I went all shaky and red; especially when I shook his hand, which was warm and wet. And the worst thing of all, on top of everything, was that when he was a man I was sort of *attracted* to him — this cop with the wet hand. When he was a woman, I hadn't felt anything at all. Well, I could feel my hand shaking and I knew I was sweating, so I decided the best thing to do was just to have it out and say what was on my mind. I mean, I would have completely freaked out right then and there if I'd had to pretend that there was nothing odd about this woman suddenly turning into a man.

He was a young man. Quite handsome, with soft features, and almost no hair on his hands or face.

I said, "Well, how are you?" Just for something to say. And he smiled that same smile. It was very sweet, but it betrayed no emotion. In fact, it turned me on. "Fine," he said. He had a very familiar voice (like the policewoman, only lower). And it made me realize how similar men's and women's voices could be. Then I just knew I had to blurt it out: "Excuse me, but this is freaking me out here. Weren't you a woman before?" And he said, "Oh yes, I'm sorry." And he sort of smiled shyly and tossed a straight lock of hair off his forehead. "I could understand how that would be odd for you. Yes, I was a woman before." "I don't get it," I said, because I didn't. "Oh I'm sorry," he said, smiling again. "In the kind of work we do, it's important for us sometimes to be in disguise." "Oh," I said, "you were disguised as a woman?" He said, "In a manner of speaking, yes."

What was this manner-of-speaking shit? I mean, was he a man or not? I wanted to ask him if he had a dick, but I knew that would have seemed rude — certainly not normal. I mean, ever since I turned gay, even though I can get turned on now and then by masculine-looking dykes, as soon as I confirm that a woman's a woman I don't want to have sex with them any more. Like I have seen totally butch dykes who really turned me on because I thought they were skinny tough boys. A lot of them have tattoos. And then I find out they're girls and my hard-on goes away.

Anyway, this was really screwing me around. I mean, what kind of shit was this? Like, before, when he was a nice woman, I felt like telling him everything. What was wrong with that? As a police tactic, it seemed to work. It sure made me want to confess. But now that she was dressed up as a man I felt an attraction, and that was fucking me up in a new, sexual way. I mean, you shouldn't want to fuck your interrogator. That's some sort of disease people developed with Nazi torturers. I'd read about it and I didn't want it to happen to me. So I was really eager to find out this person's actual gender. I asked, "What do you mean, in a manner of speaking?" And he said, "Let's just say I'm definitely a man today." Then he smiled this very sweet, sexy smile. He had nice lips. I could see him licking cock. This was really fucking me up. But I just couldn't ask him if he had a dick or not, that would seem too totally psychotic. So I decided to turn the tables on him with an old law I once read about, because I do drag. "But that's against the law, isn't it?" "Pardon me?" he said, looking up from his coffee. He'd had time to get coffee already. I said, "I read somewhere that it's against the law to wear a disguise; it's this law they used to use against drag queens." He laughed a little. I liked his laugh. "Yes, that's true. There is a law like that. But the law does not apply to policepersons."

The law doesn't apply to policepersons. I bet it doesn't. And he/she was still being as cagey as ever about his/her gender. Well if this was part of a plot to get me, I was falling for it. I was truly falling for it, because it sure seemed to me I'd like to have this guy order me around. He was a little effeminate, but only because he was so goddamn pretty. Like k.d. lang. An okay enough girl, but a really beautiful boy, you know? And then he said something I didn't understand. "Does it really matter whether I'm a man or a woman?" Well sure it matters. It completely matters. It makes all the difference in the world.

And that's when I realized that this investigation was going to be about sex. Because you see, this whole gender thing, I mean, it wouldn't have made a speck of difference, he was right, if sex wasn't an issue. If I wasn't a hypersexual person, if sex wasn't central to my whole way of being, and in fact, if my whole sex life wasn't completely wrapped up in Cassidy and this whole case, then it wouldn't really matter what gender the policeperson was. But coming out of the heat of guilt and sex and van fantasies, and being very, very hyped up because, let me tell you, I hadn't been laid in a month, which is like completely impossible for me — well, I was completely horny.

And this policeperson was making things worse. All because he suddenly turned into a man. A man who had to be pretty kinky, since he seemed to go around as a woman half the time as part of his job. And if they knew, if they knew about me and sex, and me and kink, and me and the dirty things we really did, Cassidy and me, if they found out, then my goose was cooked.

I was completely terrified, but I decided the best thing to do was to just act innocent until proven guilty. No need to get hysterical. "No, it doesn't matter," I said. But my voice quivered. And he knew it. So he smiled and said, "Okay, we can get on with it then. I'm sorry, I should have remembered that, when I talked to you before, I was the other way. Sorry." The "other way." Oh yeah, sorry. He was really sorry. He was enjoying this. So next he opens up a little pad, the same pad that he/she had before, which freaked me out, and then he said, "Cassidy is dead."

Oh fuck. Just as easy as that, he tells me. He doesn't ask me if I know. He just tells me. Very cool. Well I can be cool too. Cassidy doesn't mean anything to me. Cassidy was a stalker, that's all. An irritant. Just an irritant, that's all. If they get the goods on me, I'll say he irritated me so much I had to kill him. That's a good start. Cool.

"Oh," I say. "I didn't know that." A bit of concern in my voice. Perfectly natural. "What happened?"

"He was run over by a van. His head was smashed against the cement."

And then I did a very stupid thing. Because for a moment I felt free. I thought, if I did kill him, I didn't run over him. I just put the van in reverse and pushed him up against a wall. A brick wall, not cement. So this meant I was free. Because I didn't run him over. I didn't fucking run the wheels over his body. I was free.

I was ecstatic. I tried not to let it show on my face. I said, stupidly, oh so stupidly, eagerly, oh fuck I was so eager, "He got run over?"

And the cute policeboy who used to be a boring policewoman smiled, and it was awful. Because I knew then that I had fucked up. I knew he was very happy. He wasn't afraid to show that. The bastard. The full-lipped, cocksucking bastard. Because he was gay. I was convinced of it. He was a man and he was gay; I was sure. "Oh excuse me," he said, so incredibly happy I thought he was going to puke up his coffee. "I made a mistake there, you're right, thank you for correcting me. He was not run over. He was, in fact, pushed against a brick wall by the back of a van." Fuck. The oldest trick in the book. Catch the killer on knowing more about the murder than you do. Hadn't I seen any goddamn old movies? How could I be so stupid? And I started mumbling, "Oh... I don't know... I don't really know. I was just... I was just asking." But no. My goose was cooked.

Then he started: "Well, I'm sorry Jack." Fuck, we *were* in an old movie. The clichés were tumbling out of his goddamn sensual mouth. "I'm sorry, but we know that you killed Cassidy Blanque. Your finger-prints were found at the scene. He's dead. He told his friends that he was in love with you, that he wanted to see you. People saw a van that fits the description of Mr. Blanque's parked outside your house that night. We've talked to your friends, friends you haven't spoken to for over a month for some reason, Jack. What could be the reason for that?" (He took a little tape recorder out of his pocket. He wanted me to confess. In the goddamn restaurant. There were some of my friends, actors, theatre people, at another table. Oh well, they would think this was an interview: that

I was a big celebrity. Except that if I was a big celebrity, I was dying, shaking in my fucking boots.) "Yes, we've talked with your friends (he started the tape recorder; God, he was so fucking attractive), and it seems that your behaviour that night was very strange. You made a scene at a dinner party, yelling and doing damage to a Mr. Springfield's apartment. You then went off to visit another friend, who says that you were acting very oddly." (I couldn't believe it. Barb saying I was acting strangely? What was going on here? How could she say that about me — to the cops?) "There is no accounting for your precise whereabouts at the time of the murder. Your friend Mr. Fraticelli says that you slept at his house, something which you haven't done in, he said, and I quote, *seven years*." (Tony! They got Tony too; trust a publicist to rat on you. I never should have gone to stay there. What a mouth that guy has. He used to publicize my acting for me, now he's publicizing my fucking crimes. But this sweetie was going in for the kill. He's so obviously a top; but aren't all policemen/women tops deep down?) "So as you see, all the evidence, and it's a lot, and not all of it circumstantial..." (I can't believe he used that word, *circumstantial*. Where was the waiter? What was he doing saying this in a goddamn restaurant? Shouldn't we be at a police station? I hadn't even ordered yet!) "All the evidence points to you, Jack. So you might as well make a confession."

Jack. I really liked the way he said my name.

Now the thousandth strange thing was that I didn't feel like confessing. I mean, all of a sudden, I don't know, it was just too much like a movie, and I couldn't believe I committed this crime. I mean, I didn't even believe it myself any more. How could I have done it? I'm just a nice guy. A little guilty maybe. I've done a few bad things. Nothing major. A bit too interested in scat, that's all. I'd never kill Cassidy. I'd never *really* want to kill Cassidy. This whole thing was ridiculous. This cop was ridiculous. What was going on here? I needed to bring some reality into this situation. So I turned real cool all of a sudden; I don't know why. I had sort of lost control. Lost control in a good way. I asked him, really relaxed — and you know, I was asking myself and God, I guess, just as much as him — I asked, "Why would I want to kill Cassidy?"

"Because you were in love with him?"

Oh, here we go again. As bad as the policewoman. Why is this guy talking like a straight person? In love with Cassidy? Doesn't he know a trick when he sees one?

"I was not in love with Cassidy." And I said that perfectly believably, even with a little scorn. Because I actually believed it was true. "I was, if you want to know the truth, in love with a man named Roger." I was so proud of myself, so cool.

"We know all about Roger," he said. Boy, he was starting to really piss me off.

"If you weren't in love, well then you were sexually obsessed with Cassidy." Jesus. Where did he get this from? This policeman sure knew a lot more about gay sex than the policewoman. Fuck. What was I supposed to say now, when someone hits on the absolute truth?

Deny, deny, deny.

"I was not."

"No?" He stared at me coolly. "Well, we'll just see about that." He was beginning to sound ridiculous. But he still looked sexy. And it was his word against mine. How was he ever going to prove that I was sexually obsessed with Cassidy? He leaned across the table and lowered his voice, which was very, very sexy.

"Jack, listen to me. The courts are clogged. Trials take time and money. You know you are guilty. The tape recorder is here. We want a confession. There is a kind of relief, you know, in confessing. I don't know if you are aware of that." Of course I was aware of that — boy, was I aware of that. "All you have to do is confess, now, here, into this tape recorder, and it will be all over. Perhaps there were extenuating circumstances. Maybe a lovers' quarrel. Perhaps he hit you, or drove you to it."

Was this legal? Was he allowed to say that to me? What was the big deal about this confession? Where were my rights? Was this guy a man or a woman? This whole thing was getting too crazy.

"You can tell me all of it now. I'm listening. The tape recorder is on. Go ahead."

Well I wasn't having any of it. Fuck this. You know, at that moment I realized I would have confessed to this cute guy — there was nothing I would have liked better than confessing to this cute guy — if I was sure I'd done it. If I actually knew for sure. I mean, there was a lot of evidence. But at this point, even after years of knowing, knowing in my heart I was guilty, I still wasn't sure I did it. I don't know why. But I had to be convinced. And I wasn't going to say I did it if I wasn't 100 percent sure it was true. I stood up.

"Sorry Buddy. No confession. You want to take me to court? Go ahead, arrest me. Are you going to arrest me? Well?" It seemed to me that this guy was as freaked out as a guy in his line of work could be. He just looked at me. He said: "We have your number, Jack." Now that, I thought, was kind of funny. Did he mean my goddamn phone number? Of course they had my phone number. He had fucking phoned me. Big deal. I walked out of the restaurant.

I felt better. In fact, I didn't feel bad at all. The interrogation was over. Sure, they knew a lot. They *thought* they knew a lot. But they didn't know everything. They had no motive. And you know something, neither did I. What? I was in love with him? We've covered that one. How could I be in love with someone I thought was completely annoying and ridiculous? If I was in love with the guy, why would I kill him? And so what if I was sexually obsessed with Cassidy? That was it? That explained the whole thing? I was so sexually obsessed with him that I had to kill him? Christ, that was no explanation. And then, of course, on my way down the street, when I was thinking I had totally fooled the goddamn guy (even though he had all this evidence, and even then I was wondering if he was a real cop — because he didn't even look like a cop; he had a girl's hands, for Christsakes), just as I was feeling cocky and thinking all this, I thought of a very good reason for killing Cassidy. And that very good reason would probably be because Cassidy knew. Cassidy knew I was guilty.

And that's what was in his eyes every time I fucked his mouth. Every time he looked up at me. Every time I slapped his face. Every time he took a shit in front of me (or I took a shit in front of him). Every time. He wasn't just looking at me with some, "Oh Daddy Daddy spank me" S&M thing in his eyes; when he was looking up at me what was in his eyes was, "You're guilty. I know you're guilty." And that's the truth about me, and Cassidy knew it, and that's why I had to kill him.

Amazingly enough, when I figured this out, I almost ran back and told that stupid cop/person.

Because things had changed in a major way. It was like, now, the cop and me, we had a sort of relationship.

It had started when the officers first came to interview me, when they were women. Only I wasn't as conscious of the relationship, because it wasn't sexual. But now that the relationship was sexual, and the guy really turned me on, I wanted to see his dick. What kind of a dick would he have with those girly hands? A little one, like a kid? That would be sexy. Or maybe a real surprise; a big one. You would never expect it, because he looked so much like a girl. And maybe he was shaved — nice and shaved, and for sure uncut. (I don't know why, but I thought uncut, for sure.) All this was going through my mind because I wanted to fuck that cop now and he wanted to fuck me.

I know that's hard to swallow, but it's true. I knew it was true. But more on the level of being professional. In fact, I'm not saying it was *totally* professional. Like, if he put his dick in my mouth it would be some sort of confession of guilt on my part. I don't know what his reason would be for wanting me. I'm not saying he was in love with me either. I'm saying that he had set up a sexual relationship with me, for whatever reason (maybe even in order to catch me), and now we were tied together. And like a guy who's tricked once, and it's been very good, maybe some rough sex has happened, maybe a little mess has been made, maybe most of a hand has gone up somebody's ass, you know the sex is going to be hot and you're hooked: you're back again for more.

It was like we were gonna have another date. And he had my number. And I wasn't guilty: I wasn't tortured, I wasn't scared, I wasn't nothing. This was going to be sexy, and I was just a guy between dates. Waiting for that phone to ring, waiting for that call.

So I went home, and the first thing I did was put on the ringer on my phone, took it right off call for-warding, you know. I wanted it to ring. And I knew it would. After all, he said he had my number.

Well the phone didn't ring and it didn't and it didn't. Which really annoyed me. I mean, you'd think some of my friends might have called and apologized for fucking ratting on me. But of course I realized it was ridiculous to think that. I was a suspected murderer. I didn't have any fucking friends any more.

All I had was my cop, and a cute one at that. So I put the phone beside the bed. That's something I never do. I never want to be disturbed at night, like that night when Cassidy and I did it at the theatre and then he got strangled. I just turn the phone off whether I've had a bad fuck or a good fuck, a good date or a bad date (Cassidy's case), but this was different. This was going to be the biggest bestest date I ever had. This cop was going to fuck me, and I hardly ever get fucked. Fucked by this beautiful boy, yeah.

I went to sleep eventually. I never thought I would. I didn't even dream that I was guilty, which was odd, because I was sure in the middle of it all now. I think I was just having one of those silly "I can't remember my lines and I'm on stage" theatre dreams; I mean tense, but not crazy. And like, you know all the time you're having a dream. Maybe I wasn't even asleep at all, I don't know. And then, of course, the phone rang. It was 4:30 in the morning. At first I was freaked, scared just by the ring. Then I remembered, oh yeah, it's my date. It's my guy. My boy; my cop. And what perfect timing. I mean, 4:30 is what they call the dead of night. Everyone, even the rubbies, has gone to sleep and nobody, not even the hard-nosed business types, are at work. It's nowhere time. It was still cool, I knew because my apartment window was open, but there was no breeze. So still. Just that ring. From my sexy new cop boyfriend. I picked up the phone. "Hello?"

"Hello, Jack." (Oh fuck, his voice was so smooth, he could make me come just like that.) "How are you?" (I played it cool, like you always do, when a hot date calls.) "Sleeping." "I hope I didn't disturb you." (Smooth bastard.) "It's okay." "Were you having a good sleep?" (I can't tell you what it was like, the sound of his voice, but I knew he wanted me.) "I was dreaming about forgetting my lines." (Again, so cool, I was just having a normal theatre dream. I wasn't wanking off about him or anything.) "So Jack, I have a proposition for you." (A proposition, here it comes, he's going to ask me to meet him somewhere. This could be my whole fantasy. I was going crazy. Maybe he was just canning the whole investigation; maybe he was just so hot for me, the way people sometimes get hot for killers.) "What's the proposition?" (I wanted to sound a little interested.) "I think you and I are thinking the same thing right now." (Oh my God, it was just like phone sex. If he asked me if I was thinking about his dick, I would say yes. I would just say yes.) "Maybe." (I was still cool.) "We're both wondering whether or not you're guilty. Now we have some pretty solid evidence, but you're right Jack, you're absolutely right. We need a motive. And the motive might be that Cassidy knew something about you that was so horrifying to you, so upsetting, that you didn't want anyone to know. And you were afraid that he was going to blackmail you." (Now he's starting to lose me. Blackmail? What are we, in the 1950's? Suddenly he's being a corny cop again, and these cops are all the same. What would Cassidy have to blackmail me about, for Godsakes? I'm a drag queen and a fucking out whore gay man. What could he say about me in public?) "Or something." (What did he mean? Blackmail me — or *something*? This was stupid.) "Or maybe he just knew things about you Jack, things you didn't want anyone else to know." (Exactly what I had decided today, but this blackmail stuff just turned me off. I was tired and thinking I might just hang up the phone and go to sleep, but I asked him anyway.) "Like what?" "Oh, I don't know Jack, maybe things that you like to do in bed." "In bed?" (I sounded kind of scornful. God what do they teach these policepersons? How many homosexual perverts — maybe even killers — like me, actually have sex in bed? We have sex everywhere, not just beds.) "Maybe not just in bed." (Hey wait a minute, what did he know? I decided to ask him.) "Hey wait a minute, what do you know?" "We know a lot about you, Jack." (I strung him along, because he was sexy and he had a nice voice.) "Like what?" "Let's see now, for one thing…" (He was actually reading from a notebook. I was a fucking suspected killer, couldn't he get his Goddamn act together? Reading from a notebook! I almost hung up!) "For one thing, you showed your asshole to Barb." (Now this I could not believe.) "What?" (I could not believe that she told him, and I could not believe that it would make any difference to the police.) "So what?" (But I was shaken by this Barb thing. It always shook me in a strange way.) "And…" (He was obviously reading from the goddamn notebook again.) "And… we know that you wanted Cassidy to take a shit in that big white van." (Fuck. How did they know that? How the fuck did they know that?) "How did you know that?" (I had to ask.) "Oh we know everything about you. We know that you like to be humiliated. We know that you like to be spanked. We know that you like to get down on your knees and suck cock. We know that you like to get pissed on and spit on. We know you like to take it like a boy, like a pig. Am I right? Am I right, boy?" (Oh my God, his voice was so goddamn sexy, I just wanted to let him talk. I just wanted him to talk now, and he did.) "So we've come up with a little plan. It's a thing we do just for little sexpigs like you. We have a special secret police division that no one really knows about. It's a special international group of cop/persons, and these people are trained in the art of flagellation and humiliation and torture. We have assigned two specially trained experts in sexual torture to your case. Hans, and his young lover, Wolfie. Hans and Wolfie are waiting for you in a house on Dunn Avenue. They will test you Jack. They can test you to the core, if you know what I mean. We want very much to see how you react when being manipulated by a pair of seasoned sex professionals who will know how to fulfill your deepest desires. Hans and Wolfie are waiting for you now, at 16 Dunn Avenue. Ring the front doorbell. Hans will pay for your cab. Have a nice time. Oh, and don't worry Jack. I'll be watching."

He hung up. Fuck, I could not believe this. I mean, this guy was obviously not a policeman. This was impossible. What special force? This sounded like a bad porn movie. One with Jeff Stryker saying, "Suck it, you faggot." But then again, of course, it did hit me that if the police were going to set up a sexual investigation, then they *would* come up with something called "Special Forces — Sexual Torture Division." They would come up with a corny idea like that. (And they'd use the word "torture" not really knowing shit about S&M and consent and all that stuff.)

Hey, if you wanna know the truth (and I'm sure you do), even though I thought this whole thing was ridiculous, I was very turned on. I mean, suddenly I forgot about Cassidy. Even about the murder. I was right. This faggot cop man/woman was out to get me in bed. And he sure knew the right buttons to push.

In fact, maybe my special status as a perverted sex murderer was going to put me in contact with more people like this; at least I hoped so. Fuck, this was crazy. I mean, you'd think I would have been totally paranoid, thinking, "How did these guys figure out what I liked to do in bed? How did they know my exact fantasies? Why did they care if I showed Barb my asshole?" But everything was so crazy now, that it seemed like maybe I was still dreaming. And this was a fucking hot dream. I mean fuck, before I'd been dreaming about being in *The Importance of Being Earnest* and forgetting my lines.

And then, in another way, it didn't seem strange to me at all that this cop knew everything about me. As I've tried to explain, I always thought everybody knew everything about me anyway. I even thought they hated me for it. So it sort of made sense. I mean, maybe if the cops couldn't get me for being a gay activist, they could get me for Cassidy's murder. And if they couldn't get me for Cassidy's murder, then they could get me for having sex with Hans and Wolfie. Which was the thing I was really starting to relish being guilty of.

Fuck, I had to get going. Hans and Wolfie were waiting. I know I'm going to get into a lot of trouble for saying this (it's so politically incorrect) but just let me tell you that if any gay man anywhere got this call saying that Hans and Wolfie would be waiting for them, they would be out of that door and down to 16 Dunn Avenue faster than a fart out of a cat's ass.

I pulled on a jockstrap. It was my favourite sex gear. I have this one with a knitted pouch that makes my dick look gigantic (it *is* pretty big), and if the cop was going to be watching (fuck, he said he'd be watching, and it made me so horny!), then I wanted to look fabulous. I brought some poppers which I had kept hidden when I started dating Roger. (I was going to throw them out, but something stopped me; little did I know that I would need them for Hans and Wolfie.) I was ecstatic, I was totally ecstatic.

I practically jumped out of my apartment and headed down the street. I didn't bother to put on a shirt. I don't know how I got a cab to pick me up; I must have looked nuts. But I felt great. I didn't have any money. You know, I almost threw my fucking house keys out the window of the cab, that's how crazy I felt.

The cab driver didn't say a word; he was kind of ugly and he looked like he'd had a very bad night. He was one of those sad late-night cab drivers. I thought, "Boy, this guy would be the perfect guy to drive you to your fucking death."

Then I thought that was too scary a thing to think. But fuck, what I wouldn't do to satisfy the feeling in my dick. It was getting hard against the woven jock. Just thinking about Hans and Wolfie was killing me. I hoped they were eastern European. Maybe German. Or Polish. Very dominant and filled with anger and bitterness about the Second World War. I didn't want any swastikas or anything. Just two pissed-off sexy guys with big uncut dicks who would make me feel like shit.

I had a feeling that anything I imagined in that cab, on my way to Dunn Avenue, would for sure happen that night.

When I got to the house it really turned me on. It was an old Gothic place, gigantic and sort of menacing, like the house in the movie *Psycho*. Just what I had imagined, actually. The cab driver didn't mind waiting; he looked like he was sleeping, or even dead. I practically bounced up the steps and banged on this old knocker. It was like something out of a freaky porn movie: just scary enough.

Hans opened the door. Wow. Like, all I have to say is: *Wow*. If I had to imagine the perfect older guy, it would be him. Now I have never been into older guys (they scare me because they all tend to be so much like Denton: very fucked up. Like I said before, a lot of older gay guys have had very fucked up lives and it shows), but I would certainly make an exception in the case of Hans. Actually, he didn't say "Hello I'm Hans" or anything. He didn't say anything at all. He smiled and handed me the money. How did he know how much?

I ran down to give the cab driver the money and turned back to look at Hans. (I figured all the neighbours were asleep so they wouldn't see me looking at him.) Fuck. Hans was standing there wearing nothing but chaps. He was one of those older guys who has a bit of a hairy gut, but it was oh so big and hard and sexy. You just wanted to lay your head against it or suck right on his big innie bellybutton. He had two big piercings (one in each nipple), and a big Prince Albert on his dick. What a chest. Really hairy. And big hairy legs. And I just knew he had a big hairy butt. Of course he had facial hair, which usually turns me off, but this Hansie pulled it off. And what a Polish sausage. And what balls. That was the most amazing thing about Hans, actually, when I look back on it. He had this gigantic bag, which he had shaved. And he was wearing a cock ring, of course, and this huge bag of balls just sort of hung there on his thigh, like, well, begging me to shove it in my mouth. I just loved those balls. I bet I could barely get the two of them in my mouth. I mean, if he swung those balls at you and hit you in the head, he could probably knock you out. I had a hard-on as hard as a rock, which I, like, never do.

"Hello, Jack." That's what he said. And you know, he sounded both like the best warmest dad you ever had, and someone who knew all your dirty secrets. I asked Hans if I could take a sniff of poppers. He said to go right ahead. I hadn't done poppers in months. I wanted to savour this whole thing completely. He closed the door and led me through a hallway which was covered, as I expected it to be, with erotic art. (I mean I could have designed this place, for Christsakes!) When he turned around I also got a good look at his butt; it was hairy all over, and huge. Boy, I wanted to get my nose in that.

The stuff in the hallway was really beautiful. Sculptures and paintings and stuff. I mean, some rich perverted fag obviously owned this house and had lent it to them. Or maybe Hans was the Rich Fag himself.

"How are you feeling, Jack?" Jesus, this whole thing was obviously going to be about how I was feeling. Everything was going to be about how I was feeling. I let him go ahead of me as he turned the corner. It was something else watching his big butt quiver and shake as he walked. Hans was obviously proud of his big butt. And well he should be, too. I told him I was feeling fine. I had all these feelings welling up inside. I mean, besides my hard-on. I felt like a big man and a little boy all at the same time. I actually took off my pants in the hallway. I just threw them on the floor. That's how great I was feeling. I asked Hans if he minded me doing that.

"You can do anything you want, Jack. As long as you're ready to be a big sexpig." God, he said exactly the right thing. And just the right way too. If he had said "little sexpig," it wouldn't have turned me on. But no, he said "big sexpig." And that's what I felt like: big and sexy and hard. I was so horny.

We got to this door that I figured led to the kitchen, and I thought, "Why is he taking me to the kitchen?" And then he opened the door and I saw that there was a lot of white light. Then I realize that the whole room is white. Fuck. Actually, it looks like it could have been a kitchen once. Now it looked a little bit more like a toilet. In the sense that there were toilets in certain places around the room. An enema bag was hanging from the ceiling. On one wall were some gigantic dildoes. But the most amazing thing of all was on the table, in the centre.

There was a very white table in the centre of the room. It was padded. And lying on the table was a beautiful young guy.

Fuck, he was beautiful; he was like my perfect guy. He was naked, of course, and he was lying face down. What made him so perfect was his hair distribution. He had some nice blond hair on his head, I liked that. (Hansie's head was shaved.) But on his body he had this great fur that covered his legs and his fantastic ass. Oh what an ass he had! And his hair on his head was obviously dyed because on his legs and ass the hair was thick and dark and curly. That kind of hair that covers your legs and ass like a fawn. And just at the top of his butt-crack it stopped in a perfect line. Like he was part boy, part animal. The main thing about his ass was that it was so damn big. Not flabby, just gigantic. Like some boys just have these asses that are far out of proportion to their bodies. I mean, his ass was huge, even though his legs were big too, and muscular. And the hair was so dark going into his crack, I just wanted to go in there. His legs were spread so you could see the hair coming out of his crack.

The amazing thing about the table was that it was sort of raised up, and it had a hole in it. Wolfie was tied down to it, of course. Spread-eagled, as I said, on his stomach. The hole in the table was being used for his dick right now, and it was massive. It wasn't fully hard, but it was bigger than Hans's. It was hanging like this huge slab of meat, and I guess it was partially hard because the head was exposed. And the strange thing was... I guess I should stop saying that now. Because none of this stuff was strange any more. It was exactly what I wanted.

His cock was pointing down into a toilet, located directly below the bed. He could pee into the toilet, and also, somebody could sit on the toilet and suck him off. Wolfie also had a hole where his face was, and the table was slanted down towards the front a bit, so he could look at his own dick. Just as we came in, Wolfie started to talk.

"Fuck, Hans, I can't hold it any more!" "You can't hold it? Just a little longer?" "No Hans, please, I just got to take a piss." (He had this great sort of surfer boy voice, Wolfie did. He sounded like Keanu Reeves or something.) "Okay, you piss like a good boy. Go ahead." So Hans flicks a switch, and the lights in the room, I swear, they changed all of a sudden so there was a spotlight just on Wolfie's dick. And all the other lights in the room dimmed. His dick and the toilet. And Wolfie's face was kinda screwed up because he was, like, letting the piss go. And sure enough Wolfie pissed right in the toilet and he looked so relieved and moaned as he was pissing. His big hairy ass moved up and down with relief too. "That's a good boy," said Hans. "Good boy." "Oh, oh yeah. Fuck, shit that's good. I needed that." He looked so relieved. I felt better for Wolfie. So Hans turned to me. "This is Wolfie. Jack, Wolfie. Wolfie, Jack." "Hi man," he said. He seemed a bit embarrassed. Like a surfer dude caught with his pants down and his big ass showing.

Which, of course, is exactly what he was.

So Hans turns to me: "So, Jack, I hear you're quite the sexpig." "Yes I am sir." "So why don't you show us what kind of a sexpig you are?" "Yes sir." "Why don't you just show us your ass?" "Yes sir." (As he was saying this he was letting Wolfie loose. Wolfie was just like this big surfer kid — muscled stomach, small hairless perky pecs, that great little line of hair going down from his pierced navel to his hairy ass and legs.) "Here we go; help me Wolfie." So they take a hold of me and lead me over to his bed thing. And they lay me down on it, and Hans pulls off my jockstrap so I'm completely naked. I never felt so naked in my life. He pushes a button, and this mirror comes down from the ceiling, and I see it's made just so I can look in another mirror that's in front of my face: so if I'm lying flat on the bed I can see my ass perfectly. "That's good." "You got him Wolfie?" (Wolfie seems proud of himself.) "Yes sir." "You had a great piss, didn't you?" "Yes sir." "Good boy." "Hey, Jack's got a great big smooth pig's ass, doesn't he?" (Wolfie seemed to like my ass.) "Yes Wolfie, smooth like you like. Let's have

a good look at it." I could hear him flick a switch and
the lights went down. Everything was black; the only
light was on my asshole. I could also see Wolfie's cute
young face, and I could see his hand go down to his
big, heavy dick like he was going to frig himself.
"Now let's just have a good look at Jack's asshole."
(God, this was so embarrassing, but I wasn't really
embarrassed at all. I was completely hard, and big.) So
they aim this light right at my hole, and I can see the
light, and well, it's a very different sort of thing to do.
Because, well, I don't know if you've ever noticed, but
it's very difficult to get a good look at your own asshole.
It's almost impossible. But there I was, staring down at
the floor and I could see Hans's hairy hands kneading
the flesh. He was kinda kneading my ass, and he was
starting to put in his greased-up finger. It felt great. He
put one of his fingers all the way in. Fuck, his fingers
were big. And then he started to move his finger
around, in a nice gentle way, but strange. It was as if
he was cleaning out my asshole. As if he was gouging
it out. Like, cleaning out all the shit. "What are you
doing?" (I asked him, but I knew.) "I'm cleaning out
your hole boy, it's kinda messy. Look at that Wolfie!"
(He took out what looked like a tiny brown turd and
held it up to the light.) "Look at that Wolfie."
(Wolfie looked very happy and started to jerk off very
hard.) "Let me have some!" (He said that just like a
kid asking for some dessert. I couldn't believe it. Then
Wolfie just sort of climbed on the back of the table. It
had some sort of extension which came out of it; and
even though my legs were really spread, they raised
the table a bit more, so that my ass was in a better
position for him to reach it with his mouth, and then
he, well, he chowed down. I could see him in the mirror.) "Tastes great," he said to me. "Your ass tastes

great, Jack." And it's true, he sure did seem to be enjoying it. His face didn't get all shitty or anything. In fact, I was surprised at how clean I was. But he was just burying his head in my ass. The table was made so I could reach around and jerk myself off, so I started doing it. But Hans came over right away. "Hey, boy, let me help you with that." (He got underneath the table and sat on the toilet and started to suck me off and jerk himself off while Wolfie was still chomping away. I could see Hans's big balls hanging down in the toilet as he frigged himself. Fuck, they must have been touching the water, dangling there.) "Mmmmgood," said Wolfie, like it was a Mars bar or something. He was really smiling now, and he looked shitfaced, even though his mouth was really clean. But then I got an idea.

And of course it was the idea I'd had all along. The one I'd had from the time I'd read that first story in *Drummer*. It was like I was ready to cross the line or something. It was like I knew all along with Cassidy what it was all about. I just wanted to try this whole shit-eating thing. I mean, Wolfie was practically doing it now. Look at him, he sure looked healthy. And I realized that Wolfie could lie on the table on his back and take a shit on my face, and I could sit on the toilet underneath the table and he could use me as a toilet and I could jerk off.

Wolfie, of course, was one of those boys who had such a big hairy clean ass that his shit wouldn't even stink. It would probably taste like chocolate.

Well that would be just too perfect. "Hey Hans," I said. "Yes boy." (He answered me, between mouthfuls of my dick.) "Do you think Wolfie would like to take a shit in my mouth?" (Before Hans could even answer, Wolfie interrupted.) "Fuck yeah. And I feel a big load coming on." (Oh this was too great. But I couldn't believe I was doing this. I just couldn't believe it. It was going to happen, and let me tell you, I wasn't so far gone that I didn't realize that that policeboy was probably watching. He was going to watch me get some shit in my mouth.) "Do you want me to tie you onto the crapper?" (Hans asked, which was very nice and convenient of him. I noticed for the first time that he did have a bit of an accent. But it sounded more Czech than German. He certainly wasn't a committed top, just committed to pleasing me, which was great. I told him no because I wanted to be able to get out at the last minute, if I thought I couldn't handle the whole shitting in my mouth thing.) "Okay Wolfie, we'll put you in the sling." (Oh fuck, they had a sling.)

So I get on the toilet, in my favourite position, and Hans lowers this great big sling. Fuck, I realized I hadn't sucked on his enormous bag yet; I'd have to save that for later. And Wolfie climbs into it. It was a great sling. It shaped Wolfie's ass so it looked gigantic and hairy, and his cheeks were wide open. Hans dimmed the lights and put a spotlight on his hole. God he had a beautiful asshole. I was hypnotized. Hans had also positioned the mirrors so that I could see Wolfie's face. "How you doin' Wolfie?" "Fine." Wolfie was fine. He looked very happy. But I could see a bit of strain on his face. "I think I feel a big dump coming." Wolfie looked so cute when he said that, kind of shy about his big oncoming dump, but eager too. "Go right ahead, Jack wants it. Right in his mouth." (I was wanking like crazy now. I couldn't believe how beautiful Wolfie's asshole was. I mean, with the cheeks parted liked that right over my face. I could see there was a lot of hair around the hole. But the hole was still very pink, like a rosebud. It was sort of going in and out gently, I wanted to touch it. I did. Wolfie groaned.) "Feel good Wolfie?" asked Hans. "Oh yeah." "Feel like you want to let loose a big one?" "Oh yeah, I gotta shit. I gotta shit bad." (It was almost ready to come now, I could tell by the expectant expression on Wolfie's beautiful young face.) "Oh yeah, here it is. I can feel it now. I can feel it coming."

It was really an amazing sight, to watch his asshole open like that, the turd just starting to come through. It was big and dark brown and at first I didn't smell anything.

Then I began to smell it and everything changed. It was as if I suddenly realized where I was and what I was doing.

There was something about the smell.

I mean, it's not like I've never smelled shit before. We all have. But even though I'd always had fantasies about this, I just couldn't make myself — that is, I looked at it, and the look of beautiful relief on Wolfie's face, but I just couldn't get myself to... I mean, it smelled like shit! What did I expect it to smell like? It smelled like human waste. I just couldn't do it. I thought I could. But, just as it was starting to come out and be a turd, I bolted up and Wolfie just took a dump into the toilet. It was a long dump. A long smelly dump. That kid had quite a lot of shit in him. When it was done Wolfie sighed. "That feels better," he said. "Do you want to clean him up?" said Hans. "No." (I said this, watching them, fascinated. But now it was kind of from a distance). "No," I said. "It's okay." "Then you don't mind if I clean him up, do you?" (And so Hans sits down and he starts to clean out Wolfie's ass. And basically, this is not clean at all, this is real shit, and it's all over his face. And he's eating it like it's fucking cheese dip or something. And I can't believe it, and the smell, the smell is just not nice. Well, I begin to think maybe this is why human beings flush shit down the toilet. Maybe that's why we have toilets. Because this smell is just too much. And now it's filling the whole room. Suddenly, I want out. I want out now.) "I gotta go," I say. Hans doesn't get mad, but he does look at me differently than before, without desire. "Don't you like to see me eating shit?" Well, that's a stupid question. Of course I don't like it. I shout, "No!" "Why not?" (Another stupid question. Get me out of here! I want to get out. I grab my jock-strap from the floor, and start to shove it on, which is no easy task — jockstraps were not meant to be jumped into. Let me out of here. The whole place just smells like shit and Wolfie doesn't look that cute any more, and Hans looks like an old man with shit all over his face.) "I'm leaving." (I somehow struggle into the jockstrap and go to the door; but when I pull on the handle all hell breaks loose.)

I'm not kidding. All the lights go on. Bells. Sirens. My God, this must be waking up the whole neighbourhood. And then the white curtains up high around the ceiling open and suddenly you can see through them and there's people there. And for a minute I think I see Barb and Roger and Tony, but I definitely see a couple of cops, including the boycop. Except the boycop now looks like that woman again.

What the fuck is going on? Let me out! I start to pull on the door handle. Hans just sits there, with Wolfie's shit on his face. All in the line of duty, I guess. I look up again and all the cops are staring at me, except the woman cop, who is gone. I decide to stop pulling at the door. I mean, it's not doing any good. Besides, I feel like an idiot. I know I should have been surprised to see everybody up there, but at this point I wasn't surprised by anything.

Can I tell you something? When you're guilty, and you know you're guilty, you accept everything that happens to you. If people blame you for things, ultimately you know it's your fault. If people are laughing at you, or people hate you, you just think, hey, well, that's the way it's meant to be. I still basically think that the world is made up of two kinds of people: those who are guilty and those who are free. It's all a matter of how you feel about yourself.

If you're guilty you were born guilty and there's nothing you can do about it. Everything will always seem to be your fault. If your lover gets mad, you'll take responsibility. If your kid dies of heart failure, you'll punish yourself for taking him to the wrong doctor.

If you're the "not guilty" type then absolutely nothing makes you feel guilty. "Not guilty" people can treat everyone else like shit, stand people up for dates, walk all over them, screw them around, and the rest of the world is actually grateful. And why? Is it because these non-guilty people are so charismatic and sexy and charming? No, it's because they're not guilty. They simply do not accept responsibility for their actions. That's all there is to it. So there's just no point in blaming them for anything. That's what it is about these psychopathic killers. Why do you think nobody can catch them? Because they don't believe they're guilty. Which made me realize that this whole idea of me being a psychopathic killer was just romantic. I was no psychopath; I was just plain guilty. Of everything.

And I realized what being guilty was all about. It was all about having P.L. Feeley in your brain. Forever.

Perhaps I should explain: P.L. Feeley is this old guy who runs the laundromat down the street. (I know that's his name because he had a little sign up that said, KWIK KLEEN: P.L. FEELEY, PROPRIETOR.) He's ancient, ninety years old if he's a day, and really uptight. I mean *really* uptight. (Why this born-again Christian would set up his washing machines in the gay ghetto is beyond my comprehension; maybe just to get a good look at all the evil, up close.) And he's got this little area that's like "his" area at the back of the laundromat. There's pictures of Jesus Christ tacked up on the door. Not attractive pictures either, not the kind of pictures that would make me get horny and think of Cassidy. And the way he patrols that laundromat, fuck, you'd think it was the Taj Mahal. The place is filthy, and he barely drags a stinking mop over it once a day. But to him, it's like his little empire. And when you walk in there, to do your laundry, he always makes you feel like the dirtiest, sleaziest homosexual that ever lived. How? Just by looking at you. Once I put quarters in the machine and the machine ate them. So I told him and then he put his own quarters in and they worked (of course) and I said, "Sorry, it didn't work for me!" And he looked at me like, "Oh sure, you dirty asshole-sucking thief." But he just said, "I only do this once!" Like I had completely scammed him out of 75 cents. I mean, this man could make the Pope feel guilty if he was in the next room. The weird thing was that it was obvious that he was a sleazy old wanker himself. But since he's one of the "non-guilty" types I just described, it didn't matter. He could still make you feel guilty.

If you're really guilty, you've got P.L. Feeley inside your brain and you can never get him out — cause your head is just a sleazy laundromat.

All of this came to me because I had never known what it meant to be truly guilty. And now that I had actually showed all my sexual fantasies to, like, the whole world (I was sure this was on videotape and would show up on Sally Jesse Raphael's special "Home Videos That Ruined My Life" show or something), I was finally on the other side of relief. I certainly didn't think I cared any more.

When the policewoman came in (she was a woman now, and I didn't see how I could ever have thought she was a man), she was very calm and smiley and cheery. You know, I had a feeling that she was the opposite of me. The "non-guilty" kind. I mean, here's an example: she just finished dressing up as a guy and tricking some poor horny schmuck (me) into sucking ass in front of the few friends he has left in the world. But did this fucking cop feel guilty? Nope. She just wanted to get on with business.

She was wearing a suit made out of the same material as the boycop, which made me think that he had taken some kind of a serum and just morphed, which I know is a very crazy idea. She was very businesslike. This female cop didn't call me Jack any more. "So, Mr. Prat, that's that," she said as she handcuffed me. I said, "What do you mean?" Not because I cared one way or the other, but because I was kind of interested in what she was talking about. Had they found me guilty (without a trial or anything) of being a dirty wannabe (that is a fake, not even real) shit eater? Well then I was as guilty as every other fag in the world, since everyone in the world thinks we're shit eaters anyway. Even though most of us are not. She went on, "It's quite clear to us now, Mr. Prat. We have motive." (My hands were all locked up now.) "And what motive did I have?" (I wanted to know, since I was probably going to get the electric chair. Isn't that what they did to all the suspected shit-eating homos?) "Well, our experiment went exactly as we had imagined. We're pleased." (I could see she was fucking pleased; just get on with it, for Christsakes.) "This was a test; a rather elaborate one, I admit. You see, if you had lived out your wildest fantasy in front of us, then you would have been perfectly happy to see Cassidy live. But since you did not live out your fantasy, since you ran from it at the final moment, it's clear that you are still frightened of your deepest desires and longings. Cassidy represented the realization of your wildest fantasy, and so of course you had to kill him." I was going to ask her how the fuck she knew Cassidy represented the "realization" of my anything, but then I thought she probably has a videotape of Cassidy shitting on the white couch and me saying, "Hey, this is my deepest desire." Anyway, I didn't really care anymore. I just wanted to get booked. I belonged in prison. Maybe there were some sexy guys there.

She took me out in the street in my little jockstrap. I guess it's a big jockstrap actually; as I said, I weigh in at 230 pounds. I could see myself doing a lot more weight-lifting in prison. Actually, I was kind of looking forward to one of those Boot Camp places with all the sexy young skinhead guys learning how to be better people; but I had a feeling that if I escaped the death penalty, then they wouldn't send me to a wish fulfilment fantasy place like that. No, if they didn't execute me — and they didn't execute many people these days — they'd probably send me to some prison with fat old hairy ugly boring straight guys with bad taste. That would be real punishment.

Anyway, she herded me out into her little Honda

Civic and all I could think about, if you can believe it, was getting shit on her nice upholstery. Fuck me, I would always be guilty. There was no escape.

It didn't take us long to get to the police station, and I wasn't so nervous about it. I figured they'd give me clothes. And it was probably like 5:30 in the morning or something: it must have taken that long for the whole incriminating sex scene (or maybe we should call it non-sex scene; nobody came). It was one of those old police stations, like you see on TV. I figured they must have shot like a hundred episodes of *Street Legal* here. Come to think of it, I'd probably been in one or two of them. Playing some ugly street hooker. I always got the ugly drag street-hooker parts, although sometimes they just took one look at me (because I was so big), and decided they wanted some young cute guy (usually straight) to play the unfortunate victim of life's twists of fate. (Which means I pretty often lost the job. Next time you watch some crime show on TV, check out the drag queens in the lobby of the station. They're not real drag queens. They're straight actor boys, who get *all* the work on TV, just because they're cute enough to get any fucking role they want.) The place was totally empty. There was one forlorn looking cop at the desk who didn't look like he enjoyed staying up this late (his shift was probably almost over). There was nobody, nobody, in the fucking place. I guess it was too early in the morning for normal crime.

The loser behind the desk looked up when the woman cop came in. Unfortunately, now that the cop was a woman again, some of my mother-associations were coming back. Nothing like being led in a jock-strap to be booked for an unsuccessful shit-eating attempt by your mother figure.

"Hi Mare," he said. As if she was fucking Mary Tyler Moore. He didn't blink an eye at the fact that I was in a jockstrap and probably smelled of shit. I'm sure I'm a much more respectable convict than I can imagine.

"Hey Stew," she said, like she brought in wannabe shit-eating killers every goddamn night of the week. "Book him." This was getting more like a made-for-TV movie every second.

"Charge?" said Stew, who I noticed was chewing something. Probably Nicorette. He had the greasy yellow look of an ex-smoker, like me. "Murder," she said. Well at least she didn't say I was a wannabe shit-eater. When she said it like that it sort of sent a chill down my spine, though. Because all of this hadn't really sunk in. I think part of the reason was I was still recovering from what had been an exciting, if disappointing, sexual experience. Also, I was truly surprised that I wasn't being booked just for liking boys' assholes so much. Honest.

"Okay buddy." (I wondered if Stew would have been so chummy with me if he knew the type of murderer I was. In fact, reality was slowly beginning to hit me. I mean, didn't the criminals who committed sexual crimes get badly treated in the clink? I didn't want to be raped unless I really wanted to be raped, if you know what I mean. This whole thing was looking a lot less like a dream and starting to get scary.) "Gimme your I.D. and all your jewellery and valuables." "I don't have any I.D.," I said. I was surprised I could still talk. Stew looked up at me for the first time. He had a very weathered face, like a rubby. Big dark circles under his eyes. "Come on Buddy," he said, tired, still not at all freaked out to see me handcuffed in a jockstrap. "Don't you even have a driver's licence?" "No," I said, not even thinking about it, honest, completely casual.

And then I said, "I don't drive." He looked at me really shocked. "You don't drive?" This was the reaction that all heterosexual men had when I told them. I mean, to most heterosexual men this was the most shocking thing in the world. Well the truth is, while all these guys as teenagers were mad to get driver's licences, I just didn't give a fuck about having one because I didn't give a fuck about dating chicks, and on top of that, driving was just a very macho thing which didn't appeal to me in the least. Then it hit me, as they were both staring at me, 'cause "Mare" seemed a bit shocked by this too: *I didn't drive.* I just said it. In fact, I said it out loud again. "I don't drive. Did you hear me?" I said, really pleased with the sound of my voice for the first time in a long while. "I don't know how to drive. I never learned how to drive. Do you know what that means?" Neither of them seemed too impressed, but I was very excited. "No," sighed Mare, but she *was* a little interested. "That means that I could not possibly have killed Cassidy, because whoever killed Cassidy must have known how to drive."

"Nice try Jack," said Mare, who suddenly for some reason used my first name again. I swear if she suddenly morphed into a man again I would kill her. "You didn't actually drive. You just backed over him. Anybody can do that." "No, you don't understand!" I was very excited now. "I don't know a fucking thing about driving. I never go behind a steering wheel. I had driving lessons when I was sixteen. I failed the lessons. They wouldn't even let me take the test. They said some people are just not meant to drive a car. I would never even go behind a steering wheel.

I'm terrified of driving. I'm afraid I'd kill someone."

"Yeah, you did," said Stew. I think he thought that it was a good joke. He was a really sad person. "No, listen to me. I'm saying I don't even know where an ignition is. I *might* be able to start a car, but I don't know a driveshaft or a throttle from a crankshaft. I mean most vans have gears or something or a gearshaft, right?" Mare didn't look too happy. I could tell I might be right. "Sure they do. You have to be able to at least drive, in order to drive a van. I would never know how to start the thing, much less put it in reverse." "Then maybe the vehicle went out of control," said Mare. I was surprised. She seemed to be losing control. Now *I* was the lucid one. Standing there, in handcuffs, in my jockstrap, I was suddenly very lucid. Maybe it's because I'd been in a jockstrap and handcuffs before, just for fun, so it wasn't such a strange thing for me, ultimately.

No, I couldn't believe it. I couldn't believe my good fortune, and I really couldn't give a fuck what Mare or sad old Stew thought. I DON'T DRIVE. I DON'T KNOW HOW TO DRIVE. The words were like magic. They were singing in my head: I DON'T DRIVE I DON'T DRIVE I DON'T DRIIIIIIVVVVE! It was like an opera. Maybe they hadn't figured it out. But at the very least all I could get was manslaughter. Because I definitely would never have known how to put a van in reverse. But I really didn't even know if I had gotten into the van, let alone behind the steering wheel. Maybe that's why that part of the whole night always seemed so strange and foggy. Maybe I didn't even get in the damned van.

And then things got really clear.

I'm this guilty guy and everything. I think I'm guilty of everything. Well, maybe when I realized how much Cassidy represented my darkest desires (like the cop/person said) and how much I wanted to kill him, I just took on the guilt of killing him because of my Christian upbringing and my general guiltiness. It's certainly possible. I might have hit him, but I probably just dreamed killing him because I'm such a guilt freak. I mean, it's much less likely that I rammed him against the wall so expertly. Just think about it. I DON'T DRIVE.

Oh those yummy magic words!

So I said goodbye to old Mare and Stew. I did. I just walked out of the goddamn police station. They didn't say much. Stew was just glad to go back to his general depression, but Mare said something like, "Excuse me. Mr. Prat, you can't do this." But I went, "Sure I can. I can do anything I want. I didn't murder Cassidy. You think I'm guilty, but you're going to have to try again."

It was a wonderful feeling. I mean, I have to admit that I wasn't completely sure that I didn't kill Cassidy, but this whole driving thing threw a new light on the situation. Christ, why didn't I think of it before? Why hadn't I realized I don't drive? Well, because I was overwhelmed with guilt, that's why. Because I knew I *wanted* to kill Cassidy so much.

The night was really cool, that last cool before the cold clear light of day, which was just starting to break over the horizon. I knew exactly where I wanted to go. I didn't want to go home. I wanted to go to Cawthra Park.

I don't know if you know Cawthra Park, but it's our little gay park and it's got this AIDS memorial and everything. Trees planted by dead fags and little park benches dedicated by the leather community and stuff. It's very gay. And people have sex there and walk their stupid little hypocritical dogs there.

It's my favourite place.

It didn't take me long to get there, because the park is pretty close to the police station, and the streets were deserted. I didn't care if anyone saw me anyway. And I wasn't surprised that Mare didn't chase me.

That wasn't her style. She would just lay in wait for me; because, after all, I was guilty. And some other time she would pounce and (I was feeling very philosophical now) I'd either be ready or I wouldn't. But I'd *deal*.

The park was really beautiful. It was also very bright because the fucking city had put in these huge klieg lights to stop the homosexuals from having sex. So it was kinda lit like a football field. Of course the lights didn't stop fags from having sex. Nothing can stop fags from having sex.

In fact, there were two fags fucking behind the AIDS memorial when I got there. I decided to sit right near them, just to bug them: it seemed like a fun thing to do. I thought it was great they were having sex out in the open. A lot of prissy Denton-type fags get upset when fags fuck behind the AIDS memorial, but I always say, more power to the sex fiends. Sex is magic, sex is holy. Spill your seed, I say. It's a nice way to baptise a corpse.

They sure were making funny noises. It sounded like one of them was giving a really good blowjob, 'cause there was that telltale slurping sound; plus the other guy was saying things like, "Oh yeah, do it. Yeah, yeah, yeah." It was a very pleasant sound, and relevant, I thought, to the new day and the birds chirping and everything.

Then I think one of the fags got scared because I coughed. I heard one go *shhh* and then I heard a rustle (pants being pulled up, the leaves). Then I saw a skinny fag run out from behind the bushes. Ahhh, home again. After a few minutes the other fag came out from behind the AIDS memorial. He was kinda sexy, actually. He was heavy-set, with this baseball cap and the most piercingly beautiful eyes. I could really see them with the klieg lights on. He looked at me like he wanted to fuck my mouth. I looked back. I must have looked pretty great wearing only my jock-strap and handcuffs.

He walked up to me, giving me this piercing stare. It was great. "Hey buddy," he said. I love it when fags call me "buddy." It's so butch and friendly. I find it sort of insulting when straight guys do it though.

"Hey buddy, I'd love to fuck your face." I stared at him. He was so fucking cute.

I glanced across the street. Some sweet boy was walking by, probably on his way to an early morning shift at work. He was wearing a clean white shirt, probably fresh out of P.L. Feeley's Kwik Kleen. All I could think of was: *Now what a crying shame it would be if he got that shirt dirty.*